30 WILD AND WONDERFUL
MATH STORIES
TO DEVELOP PROBLEM-SOLVING SKILLS

30 WILD AND WONDERFUL
MATH STORIES
TO DEVELOP PROBLEM-SOLVING SKILLS

DAN GREENBERG

S C H O L A S T I C
PROFESSIONAL **B**OOKS

NEW YORK · TORONTO · LONDON · AUCKLAND · SYDNEY

Designed by Jacqueline Swensen
Cover design by Vincent Ceci
Cover and interior illustration by Rick Brown
ISBN 0-590-49169-5

To the kids
D. G.

CONTENTS

INTRODUCTION

WELCOME TO WILD AND WONDERFUL MATH STORIES

This book is designed to help you help your students become motivated and successful problem solvers. The math lessons are in the form of stories, which makes them:

- Fun!
- Funny!
- Engaging!
- Interesting!
- Challenging!
- Stimulating!

All kinds of students can benefit from this book, including:

- Students who love stories.
- Students who need high-interest material.
- Students who are highly motivated.
- Students who are not always highly motivated.
- Students who think math is no fun.
- Students who think math is fun, but are not always effective problem solvers.
- Students who don't see the purpose for the math skills they learn.

THE BOOK'S COMPONENTS

THE STRATEGIES

This book is divided into five chapters—each of which introduces one of the major problem-solving strategies.
Those strategies are:

- Guess and Check
- Use Easier Numbers
- Draw a Diagram /Make a Model
- Make a Table/Organize a List
- Work Backwards

Each chapter contains several stories with follow-up problems that can be effectively solved with the aid of the featured strategy.

Don't look for *all* the problems in the story to be solved by that strategy, though. That wouldn't be realistic. And it wouldn't take into account the fact that almost every problem can be solved in many different ways. For example, your students might choose to solve a "Guess and Check" problem by Working Backwards, Looking for a Pattern, or Using Easier Numbers. The choice is theirs.

THE STORIES

The thirty original stories in this book are packed with humor and designed to engage even the most reluctant readers and problem solvers.

Each story focuses on a combination of math concepts including:

- Multiplication
- Division
- Decimals
- Fractions
- Percentages
- Ratios
- Probability
- Patterns
- Permutations
- Geometry

To make selecting appropriate stories an easier task, the table of contents lists the primary concepts covered in each.

THE PROBLEMS

Chapters are organized by general degree of difficulty: those stories containing the easiest problems are toward the beginning and those containing the harder problems are toward the end. (Of course, *easy* and *hard* are subjective terms. Therefore, you'll probably want to decide for yourself what is most appropriate for your class.)

Individual problems range too. Some are straightforward: *How many? How much?* Others are open-ended: *How would you go about...? What would you need to know...?* Still others get to the fundamental logic of the situation: *Does this make sense? What is wrong with this approach? What do*

you predict will happen?

A variety of questions are posed for a reason: to empower students to solve the kinds of problems they will encounter in the real—and often unpredictable—world. To this end, the following are also sprinkled throughout the book:

- Problems with more than one answer.
- Problems with "messy" solutions involving fractions or decimals.
- YOUR-TURN problems, in which students are encouraged to create their own problems based on information presented in the stories.

THE SOLUTIONS

Because it's sometimes a tricky business to explain how to solve tricky problems, annotated solutions are provided on pages 93 to 106.

THE APPENDIXES

Finally, to promote effective problem solving in your classroom, you may want to photocopy "Problem-Solving Basic Truths" and one (or all) of the "Problem-Solving Top-Ten Lists" for your students. They're fun and inspiring!

HOW TO USE THE BOOK

As any good baseball hitter knows: It's easy to hit when you know what pitch is coming. What's tough about math, and problem solving in general, is that one never knows "what's coming."

The idea behind this book is to expose students to a wide variety of problems and techniques. That way, they'll acquire a basic problem-solving approach that will work with any kind of problem, regardless of whether or not they know "what's coming."

PRESENTING THE STORIES

You can share the stories with your students in a number of ways:

- Read the stories aloud. Then solve the problems together as a class.

- Photocopy and distribute the stories. Then have the students read the stories themselves and solve the problems independently.

- Photocopy and distribute the stories. Then have the students work in small groups, reading the stories and solving the problems collectively.

PRESENTING THE STRATEGIES

You might find it helpful to tell your students that problem-solving strategies are like tools. Some tools are blunt. Others are sharp. The key is to recognize that the *problem* is the important thing, not the tool.

A student should go into a problem thinking: *How can I solve this problem?* not *How can I use Guess and Check (or any other strategy) to solve this problem?*

This distinction is important.

While it is not essential that a student use the full repertoire of problem-solving strategies, it is essential that he or she be *familiar* with every strategy. Going back to the tool analogy—the more tools you have in your toolbox, the better.

TEACHING TIPS
Encouraging Words

Be Creative. If students have ideas, they should try them! Foster creativity by letting kids draw pictures, use their hands, take notes, make models, and simulate reality in whatever ways they see fit.

Combine Strategies. In the real world, this is what usually distinguishes great problem solvers from everybody else. Suggest that students use a combination of strategies. A single problem might require two or three different ones!

Conjecture. Encourage educated guesses regarding which strategy is best to use to solve a specific problem. Students should test the strategy they choose and look for signs that it is (or isn't) working.

Question. Encourage students to self-monitor their problem-solving process by asking themselves key questions such as: *Does this make sense? Is this possible? Is this reasonable? Does this fit? Can this be right?* and so on.

Consider Calculators. To help kids stay focused on problem solving—not time-consuming paper and pencil calculations—you might prefer them to use calculators.

Four Steps to Effective Problem Solving

1. ***Read the Problem.*** Make sure students carefully read the problems before they attempt to solve them.

2. ***Think Hard.*** Encourage students to really think about the problems. A strategy should soon start to emerge. If it doesn't...

3. ***Use a Pencil.*** Tell students to get their pencils going. Writing helps them think, and thinking helps them to solve problems.

4. ***Get to Work.*** Once students have settled on a plan, remind them to be systematic, be organized, and take their time.

Three Activities to Improve Problem-Solving Skills

1. ***Practice.*** To become effective problem solvers, students need to keep at it. Put another way, the best way to solve a problem is to solve another problem.

2. ***Learn from the Answer.*** If students need to peek, go ahead and let them peek. Then they can use what they've learned to solve another problem, or re-work the same problem to see "what makes it tick."

3. ***Watch Someone Else Solve a Problem.*** Better yet, have students work together. Encourage them to think out loud. Allow them to observe the way their partners operate. Listening to one another will help them learn.

GUESS AND CHECK

Frankie from Freeport has a problem. To find the batting average of his favorite baseball player, he knows he needs to divide something. But what should he divide—the hits into the at-bats, or the at-bats into the hits?

Problems like this come up all the time in the real world. Somehow, the people who are "good" in math always seem to know which choice is correct. How do they do it?

If Frankie thought a little, he would conclude that he has two choices:

1. Either he can divide 4 hits into 12 at-bats.
2. Or, he can divide 12 at-bats into 4 hits. With a limited number of possibilities, Frankie realizes that this is a perfect opportunity to use Guess and Check. He knows Guess and Check works best when:

- There are a limited number of guesses he can make.

- He knows what kind of answer to expect.

The procedure for Guess and Check

is simple. Frankie just tries something, then he looks at the answer to see whether it worked. When Frankie divides the two numbers both ways he gets:

$$4 \overline{)12.0} \quad 3.0 \qquad 12 \overline{)4.000} \quad .333$$

For a batting average, clearly Frankie's second answer makes more sense. To make sure of his method, he should try it in a few other situations, especially those in which he knows the answer.

To illustrate a different aspect of Guess and Check, here is another problem: How many hits in a row does this same player needs to raise his batting average to .500?

In this case, you can make a guess, then check your answer. If it comes out too high, adjust your guess downward. If it comes out too low, adjust upward.

If the batter gets 3 hits in a row:

$$\frac{4 \text{ hits} + 3 \text{ hits}}{12 \text{ at-bats} + 3 \text{ at-bats}} \Rightarrow \frac{7 \text{ hits}}{15 \text{ at-bats}} = .467$$

This guess is too low. We'll try 5 hits in a row:

$$\frac{4 \text{ hits} + 3 \text{ hits}}{12 \text{ at-bats} + 3 \text{ at-bats}} \Rightarrow \frac{7 \text{ hits}}{15 \text{ at-bats}} = .467$$

If a guess of 3 is too low, and a guess of 5 is too high, then a guess of 4

should be just right:

$$\frac{4 \text{ hits} + 4 \text{ hits}}{12 \text{ at-bats} + 4 \text{ at-bats}} \Rightarrow \frac{8 \text{ hits}}{16 \text{ at-bats}} = .500$$

TIPS TO SHARE WITH STUDENTS

- Guess and Check works best when you have a limited number of possibilities to try.
- Guess and Check works best when you know what kind of answer to expect.
- The key element in Guess and Check is assessment. Ask yourself: *Does this answer make sense?*

COMBINATIONS: Guess and Check works well with almost any strategy, and especially well with these:

- List What You Know
- Work Backwards
- Use Easier Numbers

CAUTION: Remind students that the Guess and Check strategy does not work well when there are too many possibilities. Also, don't let Guess and Check become a substitute for thinking. There should be a solid reason behind every guess that students make.

SPORTS BLAB WITH BUZZ BUSBY

BUZZ: Now let's go back to the phones. Frankie from Freeport— you're on WZZZ Radio-1330 SPORTS BLAB.

FRANKIE: Hiya Buzz. Love your show. I listen to you everywhere— in the car, at work, even in bed.

BUZZ: Where are you now, Frankie? I hear water.

FRANKIE: I'm in the bathtub, Buzz. That glugging noise you hear is my "Homerun" Homer Hornsby baseball bath toy. I sunk the thing.

BUZZ: Why would you want to do that Frankie?

FRANKIE: Well as you know, Buzz, I've been a big fan of "Homerun" Homer Hornsby. I wear my "Homerun" Hornsby hat wherever I go. And my "Homerun" Hornsby boots. At night I even wear my "Homerun" Hornsby pj's. But lately I'm not very happy with how He's playing. Have you calculated his batting average lately, Buzz?

BUZZ: Hmm-m. Let's see here. It appears Homer went 4-for-12 last week. That's 4 hits in 12 at-bats. What's wrong with that, Frankie?

FRANKIE: Well, here's the problem,

Buzz. When you compute "Homerun" Homer's batting average, look what you get. I divided 4 into 12:

$$4)\overline{12.0} \quad 3.0$$

You know what that comes out to? A batting average of THREE. Now, I'm no expert here, Buzz. But I figure even my CAT could hit better than that. And she's got a bad paw!

BUZZ: There is something wrong with your calculations, Frankie. And we'll try to figure out what it is on BUZZ BUSBY'S SPORTS QUIZZER. Today's QUIZZER is brought to you by the Decimal Corporation. With the Decimal Corporation, YOU get the point. And now with today's QUIZZER, here's me, Buzz Busby.

1. *Thank you, thank you. And now for today's first question. What fraction of the time did "Homerun" Hornsby get a hit?*

_____

2. *Change this fraction to a decimal. This is "Homerun" Hornsby's batting average.*

_____

3. *Homer's teammate, Terry "Big Tuna" Templeton, got 3 hits in his last 12 at-bats. What is his batting average? How does it compare to "Homerun" Hornsby's?*

_____

4. *How many hits in a row would Hornsby need to bring his batting average to exactly .500?*

_____

5. *From there, how many outs in a row would Hornsby have to make to drop his average below .333?*

_____

6. *If Hornsby made enough outs in a row to put his average below .333, how many hits in a row would he need to raise his average back over .400?*

_____

7. *What would his batting average then be?*

_____

FRANKIE:

Oh wow, Buzz. You don't know how much better I feel about this whole "Homerun" Hornsby situation. Do you know what this means?

BUZZ:

You don't need to get any new bath toys?

FRANKIE:

Or shoes, Buzz. I can keep my "Homerun" Hornsby slippers. And my hot cocoa mug. And my comb and brush set. And my "Homerun" Hornsby pocket watch. And...

BUZZ: Hold on, Frankie. I have one more question: Suppose that, from 4-for-12, Hornsby hits exactly .500 for the rest of the year.

8. *Will his batting average be over or under .500? How many hits over or under .500 will he be?*

_____

FRANKIE: Wow, Buzz. I'll really need to sit down and think about this one. I'll call you back tomorrow with the answer....If I can just remember where I put my "Homerun" Hornsby calculator....Maybe it's in my "Homerun" Hornsby desk caddy.... Bye. (CLICK)

MORRIE'S
MORE OF EVERYTHING SHOP

IF YOU DON'T SEE IT ... ASK,

In a little shop, on a little street, lived a little man named Morrie Morrison. Morrie liked to think he had everything in his shop. "From soup to nuts," Morrie said. "Whatever people want most—I've got."

For example, Morrie had 33 different types of band-aids—for elbows, knees, pinkie toes, even star-shaped band-aids, for star-shaped scrapes. And if you needed a tiny hat for your pet frog, well, Morrie had it. Or how about a chair with only two legs? Or stairs that went *down* only? Or shoes for dogs? Or a car with two steering wheels? Morrie had them all—and more.

One day an odd woman named Prudence Sneff walked into Morrie's shop. "Welcome to Morrie's More of Everything," Morrie said. "Whatever people want most—I've got. What would you like most, ma'am?"

Prudence Sneff sniffed. "What I want most, you haven't got," she said. "What I want most is time."

"Time?" Morrie said. Admittedly, he'd never had a request like this before. People had asked for hats for frogs, shoes for dogs, two-legged chairs, down-only stairs, double-wheeled cars, and star-shaped band-aids, but never before had anyone asked for anything so—well, so odd.

"Come back tomorrow," Morrie said. Then Morrie got to work. Normally, it took 7 minutes to sweep the floor. On this day, to save time, he swept twice as fast as normal. For each bit of time he saved, Morrie put a colored glass bead in a jar. White beads were worth 10 seconds; yellow beads 30 seconds; green beads 1 minute; blue beads 5 minutes; and red beads were worth 10 minutes.

1. *How long did it take Morrie to sweep the floor? How much time did he save?*

_____

2. *Which beads should Morrie put in the jar to mark the time he saved?*

_____

3. If Morrie decided to put in exactly 10 beads to cover the time he saved, which beads would he choose?

_____

Prudence Sneff came in the next day. "Where's my time?" she said. Morrie handed her the beads.

"What are these?" she asked. Morrie carefully explained to her what each bead was worth. "How do I know they're real?" Prudence asked.

"How do you know anything is real?" Morrie answered.

Prudence Sneff took a long, hard look at Morrie. Then she looked at the beads. Then she looked at Morrie again. Then the beads. Finally, Prudence smiled.

"Done," she said, shaking Morrie's hand. "Oh, and by the way," she added, "tomorrow I'll need twice as much time as I did today. Can you get it for me?"

Morrie said he could. But he didn't know quite how. His first thought was to sweep the floor twice as fast today as he had the day before.

4. How many times faster than normal would this be?

_____

5. How much time would Morrie save by doing it this way?

_____

6. Would this be enough to give Prudence Sneff the time she wanted? If not, explain what Morrie would need to do to get her the time.

_____

_____

7. Suppose Morrie saves a total of 7 1/3 minutes for Prudence Sneff. He gives her 1 red bead. What beads should she give him back as change?

_____

8. Using an equal number of each color of bead, how could you come up with a total time that can be expressed in minutes only, with no seconds left over?

_____

_____

_____

YOUR TURN

Write your own problem that involves Morrie's saving a quantity of time for Prudence Sneff. Make it a problem that has more than one solution.

WHAT PLANET AM I FROM?

MYSTERY GUEST

GRAVITY CHART			
Moon	0.16	Jupiter	2.6
Mercury	0.28	Saturn	1.2
Venus	0.85	Uranus	1.1
Earth	1.0	Neptune	1.4
Mars	0.38	Pluto	?

DICK: And now it's time to play WHAT PLANET AM I FROM? I'm your host, Dick-86. First, we'll meet our contestants. Say hello to Todd-57, Lu-26, Geri-301, and Vince-880.

PANEL: Hello Dick. (APPLAUSE)

DICK: Of course the object of our game is to use the force of gravity (*see table above*) and math to determine just which planet tonight's MYSTERY GUEST comes from. For example: If the force of gravity on Planet-X is 2.0, that means that things on Planet-X weigh twice as much as they do here on Earth. Got that, players? Good. Because it is now time to meet our MYSTERY GUEST. Sign in please, MYSTERY GUEST.

JOE: My name is Joe-09. (APPLAUSE)

DICK: We'll start the questioning with Todd-57.

TODD: Hi, Joe-09. That's an interesting last name you have. You're not by any chance related to the 09's in Fresno, are you? No? Didn't think so. Anyway, Joe, suppose I got a HALF-POUNDER burger on your planet. What would it weigh?

JOE: It would weigh about 2.24 ounces, Todd.

DICK: Pretty puny for a HALF-POUNDER, wouldn't you say?

LU: Oh Dick, you're such a card.

(AUDIENCE LAUGHS)

VINCE: Bzzzt! I'm gonna guess THE MOON, Dick.

DICK: I'm sorry, Vince-880, WRONG. The moon, last time I checked, is not, I repeat, not a planet....

LU: Bzzzt! Oh Dick, you're such a

card. (BIG LAUGH) I'm going to guess JUPITER, Dick.

1. *Is Lu's guess correct? How can you tell without even doing any calculating?*

_____

2. *What planet is Joe-09 from?*

_____

3. *How much would a 50-pound bowl of jello weigh on Joe-09's planet?*

_____

4. *Which would weigh more on Joe-09's planet, 4 ounces of styrofoam or 4 ounces of steel?*

_____

5. *Which would lose more weight on Joe-09's planet, a 10-pound bucket, or a bucket weighing 10 kilograms?*

_____

DICK: Our MYSTERY OBJECT for tonight is this dumbbell. We start the questioning with Geri-301.

GERI: Why thank you, Dick. And I must say, compared to that thing, you don't seem like such a dumbbell anymore. (HUGE LAUGH) But seriously, how much would this dumbbell weigh on Venus, Dick?

DICK: It would weigh 15 pounds less than it would on Uranus. Todd?

TODD: What about Jupiter? I've got a feeling it would weigh more there.

DICK: Right you are, Todd-57! On Jupiter it would weigh 105 pounds more than it did on Venus.

GERI: Bzzzt! I know this is crazy, Dick, but sometimes you gotta take chances. I'll guess 262.8 pounds.

DICK: I'm sorry, Geri. You're off by a mile. (GROAN) Anyone else, panel?

LU: It's like what the old maple tree said when they cut it down, Dick. I'm stumped! (BIG LAUGH, THEN APPLAUSE)

DICK: For the grand prize, the fully paid vacation to Neptune, the car, the VCR, the year's supply of plastic forks—you have one minute, contestants, to find the actual Earth weight of this dumbbell. Music please! (MUSIC BEGINS AS PLAYERS ATTEMPT TO CALCULATE ANSWER)

6. *How much would the dumbbell MYSTERY OBJECT weigh on Earth?*

_____

7. *Suppose Martians were to make a gravity chart like the one shown, giving Mars a value of 1.0 instead of Earth. What would Earth's value be?*

_____

8. *On the Martian gravity chart, which planet or moon would have a value of 2.89?*

_____

FROG GETS A TELEPHONE

Frog had a telephone installed on the old log next to his lily pad. "Ladies and gentlemen!" Frog announced. "Today is a great day. Today we become the only pond in the county to have its own telephone."

"What'll we *do* with it?" Turtle asked. "Who do we call?"

"108-642," Frog said.

"What is 108-642?" the animals asked.

Frog held up a scrap of paper. It said FRANK'S PIZZA, WE DELIVER 108-642. It was torn off right after the 2.

"We can call for pizza whenever we want," Frog said.

"We don't even know what pizza is," Turtle said.

"True," Frog said. "But I'll bet it's good. They deliver, don't they? Once they bring it to us, we'll know what it is." And he started dialing 108-642. But the number didn't work. "Must be jammed," Frog said.

But Turtle knew better. She knew that telephone numbers have seven digits. A digit had to be missing.

"Well, that's easy enough," Frog said. "We'll just look at the number and see if there's a pattern. Why, I see a pattern already." And he separated the numbers so they looked like this: 10 8 6 4 2.

1. **What pattern do you see in the telephone number?**

   _____

   _____

2. **What do you predict the next number in the pattern will be? What number will Frog dial?**

   _____

   _____

3. **If Frog dials this number, will he be certain to reach Frank's Pizza? Why or why not?**

   _____

   _____

   _____

4. **How many numbers does Frog need to dial before he is sure to reach Frank's Pizza?**

   _____

Suddenly the phone rang. "The Old Pond," Frog answered. "Frog speaking. What can I do for you?"

"Which Old Pond is it?" a voice asked.

"The one near the Old Tree," Frog said. "Over the Big Hill. Across the Muddy Creek. And down the Narrow Path."

"I'm afraid you'll need to be more specific," the voice said. "I'm calling long distance. What's your number?"

Frog threw up his feet. "Beats me," he said.

"You mean you don't even know your own telephone number?" the voice said. Frog's face turned a bright green.

"Not really," he said. "Do you know it?"

"Well," said the voice, "I know that the first nine digits I dialed were 147-126-105. And I also know that the digits in your number formed a definite pattern. But I can't recall the last number in the pattern."

"Hmm," Frog said. He wrote the number down so everyone could see it. "Does anyone see a pattern here?" he asked.

"If you can think of what the next number in the pattern is you'll have your whole telephone number," the voice said.

"Hmm," Frog said.

5. What is the next number in the pattern?

_____

6. Describe how the pattern "works."

_____

_____

_____

7. Including the area code, what is Frog's complete telephone number?

_____

8. What are the next four numbers in the pattern?

_____

The first thing Frog did after he figured out his telephone number was order a pizza. When it came, all the animals formed a circle around it. None of them thought to eat it or had the slightest idea what to do with it. Even so, they all thought it was wonderful. And from then on, every evening the animals gathered around the warm glow of a pizza and told stories in the cool night air.

9. SUPER CHALLENGE: Find the number missing from this sequence: 3 9 4 1 6 5 2 5 6 3 6 4 9. (HINT: It is one of the last three digits in the sequence.)

_____

YOUR TURN

Make up your own problem with a secret number that follows a pattern. You can use a pattern to describe another number in Frog's life, such as his locker combination, his birthdate, or his bank account.

SOAPS
• • • • • • • • • • •

Research has shown that television soap opera characters occur in the following frequencies.

Probability that a character will be:

Evil	1/2
Insanely jealous	1/3
A doctor	1/4
Wearing a hairpiece	1/8
Having amnesia	1/8
In love	3/4
Good looking	5/6
Fabulously wealthy	1/4
A fool	1/3
Heartbroken	1/9
Filthy rich	1/2
Just plain no good	1/2
A kidnapper	1/12
Well dressed	1/2
A hairdresser	1/6
A twin	1/12

1. **Quentin Crowe is a character on All the Days of Most of My Children. *What is the probability that Quentin Crowe is:***

   (A) *a doctor?*

   _____

   (B) *an evil doctor?*

   _____

   (C) *an insanely jealous evil twin of a doctor who wears a hairpiece?*

   _____

2. *What is the probability that McKenzie Beaumont on* The Long, Long, Long, Long, Long Hello *is:*

   (A) *in love?*

   _____

   (B) *filthy rich and has amnesia?*

   _____

(C) *a kidnapper with a broken heart?*

_____

3. *Of 144 soap opera characters, how many are likely to be:*

(A) *fools?*

_____

(B) *good-looking fools?*

_____

(C) *insanely jealous hairdressers with amnesia?*

_____

4. **Generally Dull Hospital** *is introducing a new character named Harley Shmelkins, whose unique combination of traits has a likelihood of 5/36 of turning up. Can Harley be:*

(A) *a hairdresser?*

_____

(B) *a fool?*

_____

(C) *heartbroken?*

_____

(D) *a doctor?*

_____

5. *How many different sets of traits can Harley have?*

_____

6. *Name the possible combinations in problem 5.*

_____

_____

_____

7. *Research has shown that real people are only half as likely to be good-looking as soap opera characters are. They are also half as likely to be "just plain no good." With this in mind, how likely is it that someone you run into by accident is both good looking and just plain no good?*

_____

8. *Other research shows that real people are 50 percent less likely to be as fabulously wealthy as soap opera characters. But they are just as likely to be well dressed. How likely is it that someone you run into by accident is both well dressed and fabulously wealthy?*

_____

THE FARMER AND THE VISITOR

A **farmer felt insulted when a** snobby visitor from another county criticized his barn.

"What's wrong with my barn?" the farmer asked.

"It's too small," the snobby visitor sniffed. "And the floor is made of dirt. Back home, our barn floors are made of smooth concrete. They're so clean you can eat off them."

The farmer decided he could do nothing to increase the size of his barn. But he could improve the quality of the barn floor. First he had it cemented over. But that wasn't good enough. He needed something to put *over* the new floor.

"How about hay?" the salesperson at the store suggested. "Hay is nice for a barn floor."

"Not good enough," the farmer said.

The salesperson brought out other coverings for the barn floor, each one more expensive than the last. To each, the farmer had the same response:

"Not good enough."

Finally, the salesperson brought in a sample of beautiful royal blue carpeting.

"Now that's what I call *good enough*," the farmer said.

The carpeting came in squares of various sizes. The barn floor measured 42 feet by 24 feet and the farmer

wanted all the carpeting to fit perfectly. He could not bear to make even one cut through such beautiful carpeting.

1. **If all of the squares are the same size, what is the least number of squares the farmer can use to cover the floor?**

   _____

2. **How large would the squares be?**

   _____

3. **If the farmer covers the floor with two different sized squares, what should their dimensions be?**

   _____

4. **How many of each type should he order?**

   _____

5. *Suppose there needs to be a layer of canvas beneath the carpeting. The canvas comes in 30 by 20 foot sheets. If the farmer could cut them in any way he liked, how many of these sheets would he need to cover the floor? (Assume he cannot use the leftover pieces to fill in gaps.)*

_____

6. *What size rectangles could the farmer use to cover the floor without doing any cutting?*

_____

7. *The farmer used 6 identical rectangles to cover the floor. What size were they?*

_____

EPILOGUE

And so the farmer installed the royal blue carpeting, which, he had to admit, looked really, really nice. In fact, it was too nice for his cows, horses, and pigs.

So the farmer built a new barn for his animals, and turned the old barn with the royal blue carpeting into an elegant country inn.

Years passed. The farmer became prosperous. Meanwhile, the visitor fell on hard times and took to wandering the countryside. One day he returned to the farmer's land. The old barn was so grand, he didn't recognize it anymore. When he asked for a free place to stay the desk clerk replied: "Why should I give you anything?"

"Because years ago, I used to visit around here," the visitor said. And he proceeded to tell the clerk the story of the foolish farmer and his luxurious barn.

"That man was my father," the clerk said. "And right now you are standing in that barn."

Just then the farmer walked in. When his son told him who the man was, a smile of delight came to the farmer's face. He handed the visitor the key to his best room and ordered him a fine meal from his restaurant.

"But why?" asked the visitor. "After I was such a snob to you, why give me these wonderful gifts?'

"Ah," said the farmer. "Because you were the one that finally convinced me that I was a fool. Before that I had only suspected it. Once I knew I was a fool, I didn't need to worry about it any more. I just did as I pleased."

And with that, the farmer left, leaving the visitor scratching his head, staring at the key in his hand.

USE EASIER NUMBERS

Victor Rappozi, who weighs 250 pounds, can lift his entire family off the ground, a weight of 480 pounds. His 150-pound wife, Magda, can lift a weight of 330 pounds. If Magda weighed as much as Victor, how much more or less than her husband could she lift?

Looking at this problem, students may not be sure how to proceed. They might think, *If only the numbers were easier, then I would know exactly what to do.*

If your students show signs of thinking this way, encourage them to follow their instincts. Have them rewrite the problem with easy numbers instead of the numbers that are there. In a sense, they will be solving two problems, one easy and one hard. Once students know how to solve the easy problem, they can use the same procedure to solve the hard problem.

The tables below show two sets of numbers, hard ones and easy ones.

HARD NUMBERS

	Victor	Magda
Body weight	250	150
Weight lifted	480	330

EASY NUMBERS

	Victor	Magda
Body weight	200	100
Weight lifted	400	300

Using the easy numbers, the problem is fairly simple. To equalize the body weights of Magda and Victor, multiply hers by the ratio of their body weights, 2:1.

BODY WEIGHT RATIO

$$\frac{\text{Victor} \rightarrow 200}{\text{Magda} \rightarrow 100} = \textbf{2:1}$$

If students double Magda's body weight, they must also double the actual amount she can lift. Doubling 300 gives them 600, indicating that Magda could lift 600 pounds.

Now that they have solved the "easy" problem, students can solve the "hard" problem in the same way. To equalize the body weights of Victor and Magda, students must multiply by the ratio of their body weights:

BODY WEIGHT RATIO

$$\frac{\text{Victor} \rightarrow 250}{\text{Magda} \rightarrow 150} = \textbf{5:3}$$

To find out how much Magda could lift if she weighed as much as Victor, students multiply the actual amount she can lift, 330, by the ratio (5:3) of their body weights:

$$\frac{330}{1} \rightarrow \frac{5}{3} = \textbf{550}$$

Magda could lift 550 pounds, or 70 pounds more than Victor, if the two weighed the same amount.

TIPS TO SHARE WITH STUDENTS

- Use Easier Numbers when the numbers in the problem are confusing.
- Substitute for some or all of the numbers in the problem.
- Make a list of the easier numbers used.
- Solve the easy problem first. Use the same procedure to solve the hard problem.
- Use Easier Numbers any time the numbers in a problem are "messy," or the relationships between numbers are unclear.

COMBINATIONS: The Use Easier Numbers strategy works well with most of the other problem-solving strategies, and especially well with these:

- Draw a Diagram
- Work Backwards

CAUTION: Students should choose simple, round numbers that they can tell apart at a glance. Make sure students remember that the easier numbers they use are temporary, and be sure they substitute the real numbers back into the problem to get their answer.

THE FABULOUS RAPPOZIS

The Rappozis were the world's strongest family. Victor Rappozi was the world's strongest father. Magda Rapozzi was the world's strongest mother. The kids were the world's strongest kids. Grandma Rappozi was the world's strongest grandma.

And wouldn't you know it. They were being recruited for the Olympic team by some skinny, know-it-all coach.

"Hello Victor," the coach said on the phone. "How would you and your powerful family like to be in the Olympics? I'd like you all to compete in the mile run."

"Hmm," Victor said. "Running isn't really our event. Perhaps we could strap sacks of potatoes on our backs..."

"No, no, no," the coach said. "As far as I know, there are no potato events in the Olympics."

"Hmm," Victor said. "How about pickles? Are there any events where you have to lift a barrel of pickles?"

"I'm afraid not," the coach said. "But I'll tell you what, Victor. Let me check to see if there's an event for your family. I'll get back to you."

That night, while the Rappozis all sat around the dinner table talking about amazing feats of strength, the phone rang.

It was the coach. "Good news, Victor," he said. "I checked the rules. There are no events with potatoes or pickles, but there *is* one event where a family has to lift itself off the ground."

"Great!" boomed Victor, "We'll be glad to participate." Then he slammed the phone down so hard that it broke in half.

The rest is history. In trial after trial, each member of the Rappozi family broke the Olympic record in the "Lifting the Rest of Your Family" event. This event requires each family member to lift every other family member who is lighter (or of equal weight) at the same time. For instance, Victor—as the heaviest Rappozi—had to lift the entire family at once in one terrific heave (*see illustration*). Meanwhile, Grandma Rapozzi (second lightest) had only to lift Baby Rapozzi (the lightest).

1. *How many pounds does Grandma lift?*

   _____

2. *How many pounds does Chip lift?*

   _____

3. *How many pounds does Rowena lift?*

   _____

4. **How many pounds does Magda lift?**

_____

5. **How many pounds does Victor lift?**

_____

6. **What is the ratio of Victor's weight to the amount of weight he lifts when he lifts the rest of his family?**

_____

7. **Rounded to the nearest whole number, how many times Victor's body weight does he lift when he lifts the rest of his family?**

_____

8. **Pound for pound, who is stronger: Victor or Magda? HINT: Base your answer on the ratio of how much each weighs to the amount each is lifting.**

_____

9. **SUPER CHALLENGE:** *If Magda weighed as much as Victor, could she lift the rest of the family? If not, who would she leave out? If so, how many extra pounds could she lift?*

_____

After they collected their gold medals, Rowena was feeling feisty and challenged her mother.

"I know something I can lift that you can't lift, Mom," she said.

"That's impossible," Magda said.

"You want to bet?" Rowena said. "If

I win, you have to teach me your SECRET POWER GRUNT."

"No way!" Magda cried. "You know you aren't allowed to learn the SECRET POWER GRUNT until you reach the age of 21. It's family law."

"What do you have to worry about?" Rowena said. "I only weigh 100 pounds. How could I possibly lift more than you?"

"Hmm," Magda said. "Maybe you're right. What do I get if I win the bet?"

"I'll never bother you about the SECRET POWER GRUNT again until I'm 21," Rowena said.

"It's a deal," Magda said, putting out her hand.

"OK," said Rowena, shaking her mother's hand. "Now I can lift you, right, Mom?"

"Right," answered Magda, looking puzzled.

"But you cannot lift yourself, can you?"

Magda thought about that for a moment, "I suppose you're right."

"All right," said a gleeful Rowena. "Now teach me that SECRET POWER GRUNT!"

SYLVESTER JAMES LEE

Sylvester James Lee
How he loved TV
Soaps and sitcoms, football games
"I love them all," said Sylvester James
He knew every show and every star's name
And it didn't matter
If it all seemed the same
"That's how I like it," said Sylvester James.

Then one day he pushed REWIND
On his VCR, only to find
A brand-new show on his TV screen:
THE PAST AND FUTURE LIFE OF SYLVESTER JAMES LEE.
Backwards he went—it was crazy and wild
To see himself watching TV as a child.

Then he pushed FAST FORWARD
And he pushed it fast
Jolting him forward
And out of the past
And into the future where all he could see
Was an older Sylvester still watching TV.

"Oh no, oh no, what a terrible me,
What a terrible life," moaned Sylvester James Lee.
"Is that all the future has in store?
What a terrible waste! What a terrible bore!"

And suddenly he knew what had to be done
Slowly he put down his remote control gun
And with his eyes filled with tears,
For the first time in years,
Sylvester James Lee
Walked over, reached out, and turned off
The TV.

"The Past and Future Life of Sylvester James Lee."

1. Suppose Sylvester James Lee's life really could be played like a videotape. If the tape counter started at zero when Sylvester was born, and read 1,220 on his 4th birthday, how long was each year?

   _____

2. What would the tape counter read on Sylvester's 12th birthday?

   _____

3. How old would Sylvester be when the counter read 1,846?

   _____

4. Suppose Sylvester wants to travel back one month in his life. How far should he rewind the tape?

   _____

5. Suppose Sylvester wants to visit the future to see what his own kids are like. Where should he stop the tape?

   _____

6. Sylvester rewound the tape below zero to the point where it read 9,900. (The tape counter goes up to 9,999.) What does this mean?

   _____

   _____

7. **SUPER CHALLENGE**: What was Sylvester's "age" in Problem 6?

   _____

YOUR TURN

Make up a problem in which you ask your audience to use Sylvester's "time machine" to turn back to some famous date in history.

NOSE JOB

It was a cold night in the town of Two-Ply. So cold that the waterfall in the Two-Ply River froze over. And the clock at the Two-Ply State Bank froze and stopped at exactly 12 midnight.

Then the unthinkable happened.

Sheriff Philamina Two-Ply didn't learn about it until the next morning. There was a rap on her door. It was her cousin Bill. He was a Two-Ply, too. In fact, most everyone in the whole town was a Two-Ply of one sort or another.

"Philamina!" he cried. "Come quick! Moses Two-Ply's nose just froze solid and fell off!"

Philamina put on her sheriff's hat and sheriff's badge and ran into town. And there it was—the statue of her great grandfather, Moses Two-Ply, the town founder and original Two-Ply— completely NOSELESS!

Underneath the statue were the remains of the nose—a pile of rubble.

"This just won't do," Philamina cried.

It wouldn't do because noses were important to the town of Two-Ply. Moses Two-Ply had made his fortune from noses. First he invented nose plugs. Then nose cream. Then nose drops. Then came his masterpiece— the two-ply tissue. Because of Moses Two-Ply, noses all over the world were happier, healthier, and better taken care of.

"What now?" Bill asked.

"Make a new nose," Philamina said.

"How?" Bill asked. "The old nose is totally shattered. How do we know what it should look like or how big it should be?"

"Hmm," Philamina said. "Turn sideways, Bill. Folks always did say you looked a lot like Grampa Moses. Especially your nose. Meet me at the statue in a half hour."

"What for?" Bill asked.

"You'll see," Philamina said.

A half hour later they stood under the statue. Philamina had a tape measure.

"It won't work," Bill said. "The statue's too tall to measure with a tape measure."

"We're not going to measure the

statue," Philamina said. "We're going to measure three things: your shadow, the statue's shadow, and the size of your nose."

Bill grabbed onto his nose.

"I can understand your wanting to measure my nose," Bill said. "But what does my shadow have to do it?"

"Hold still," Philamina said, as she measured Bill's nose. It was two inches in length, by one inch wide, by one inch deep.

The 6-foot-tall, 200-pound Bill had a 2 1/2-foot shadow. The statue had a 15-foot shadow.

"I sure hope you know what you're doing," Bill said.

Philamina just smiled. "Don't I always?" she said.

1. *"First we need to find the height of the statue," Philamina said. How can they do that?*

_____

2. *Bill is how many times as large as his shadow?*

_____

3. *The statue should be how many times as large as its shadow?*

_____

4. *How tall is the statue?*

_____

5. *What is the length of the statue's nose?*

_____

6. *How many 1-inch cubes of clay would be needed to make a nose the size of Bill's nose?*

_____

7. *About how many cubes would be needed to make a nose for the statue?*

_____

8. *If each cube of clay weighs 1/4 of a pound, how much would the statue's nose weigh?*

_____

The new nose was unveiled just in time for that year's Nose Festival. Everyone thought it was just perfect, so much like the old one that you couldn't tell the difference.

As for Bill—he walked around saying "That's my nose up there!" and turning to the side so people could see it.

Of course, most of the people at the festival were Two-Plys, and they didn't see anything at all special in Bill's nose—because they had the same nose themselves! But Bill was proud anyway. Philamina was proud too. In fact, even the old statue seemed to have a new twinkle in its eye.

And the next morning in the newspaper there was a big picture of the nose. The headline read: MOSES'S NOSE'S OKAY!

And it never fell off again.

THE EXAGGERATED NEWS

None of the numbers in the following newscast are correct. They are all exaggerated or distorted in some way.

Each paragraph contains at least one clue for correcting its mistakes. FOR EXAMPLE: Suppose one of the paragraphs claimed that there were only 30 minutes in an hour. Then you would know to multiply every number in that paragraph by 2.

All exaggerations in a paragraph can be corrected by multiplying or dividing by this "exaggeration factor."

Different paragraphs have different "exaggeration factors."

You may need to use a clue from one paragraph to find the "exaggeration factor" in another paragraph.

Cable-100 presents: THE EXAGGERATED NEWS, with CHUCK UPLEE and NOREEN SPLEEN.

CHUCK: Good evening, I'm Chuck Uplee, and this... is THE EXAGGERATED NEWS, seen nightly on over 400 channels across the globe. WE exaggerate the news—so YOU don't have to.

Our top story tonight is once again Mable Meekly's 1760-pound cat Pinky, who has been up in a tree now for exactly a week, or 13,440 hours. With more on the story, here's Noreen....

NOREEN: Yes Chuck, our old friend Pinky the cat is at it again. And strangely, he always seems to show up in presidential election years. He appeared during the last election, 44 years ago. Then Pinky held an entire family of 429 mice hostage. This time it's dogs. If the Mayor doesn't pass the new Leash Law, Pinky, whose IQ is reported to be 946, threatens to unleash his entire 3,806-pound supply of catnip on the city.

CHUCK: You don't mean—

NOREEN: That's right, Chuck— Catnip Winter. If that catnip becomes airborne by tomorrow we could have a deadly green Catnip Cloud hanging over our heads. The city's entire population of 48,750,000 cats would be out of control for all 23,250 days during the month of March. That means rolling around the floor, snatching at pieces of strings, and just generally acting like fools instead of cats. The 15,000 member City Council will have to do something.

CHUCK: Is there anything that can be done, Noreen?

NOREEN: Well, first I'd like to say that the Mayor is looking into the new Leash Law. It totaled 5.5 votes in the City Council, receiving a majority by a margin of 1 vote. But the dogs were furious about Provision 611—the new Sniffing Provision.

CHUCK: The one that requires all dog sniffing to be done within a mile radius of a dog's residence?

NOREEN: That's the one, Chuck. The dogs say it's a violation of their Freedom to Sniff, which was guaranteed in the year 444 in our U.S. Declaration of Independence. The cats say dogs do too much sniffing as it is. They spend over 15 percent of their time sniffing in a normal life span of 3 years.

CHUCK: Give us your opinion, Noreen. Who's right?

NOREEN: Well Chuck, I'd say they both can make a good case. The Dogs' Right to Sniff is being violated here. On the other hand, sniffing all too often leads to cat-chasing.

CHUCK: What do you think the Mayor's going to do?

NOREEN: We'll find out tomorrow, Chuck. Until then, this is Noreen Spleen reporting for the EXAGGERATED NEWS.

CHUCK: Thank you for that fascinating report, Noreen. And now a word about Tonight's

Midnight Movie at 10 PM: "16,666.666 Leagues Under the Sea."

Write the real, *unexaggerated* numbers below:

1. *Channels on which EXAGGERATED NEWS is seen:*

   _____

2. *Pinky's actual weight:*

   _____

3. *Hours Pinky spent in the tree:*

   _____

4. *Last time Pinky was seen:*

   _____

5. *Number of mice:*

   _____

6. *Pinky's IQ:*

   _____

7. *Number of pounds of catnip Pinky has:*

   _____

8. *Cat population:*

   _____

9. *Number of City Council members:*

   _____

10. *Votes received:*

    _____

11. *Actual provision number:*

    _____

12. *Declaration of Independence year:*

    _____

13. *Time spent sniffing:*

    _____

14. *Dog life span:*

    _____years

15. *Time of Midnight Movie:*

    _____

16. *Movie title:*
    (Hint: Round to the nearest whole number.)

    _____

THE CIRCLES

In a small, round town on a circular planet in a ring-shaped house on a hoop-shaped street lived the Circle family. There was Pam Circle, Bob Circle, and Danny Circle, their son.

"Wake up, lazy bones!" Pam Circle said to young Danny who was snoring away in his circular bed.

"Aw Mom," Danny Circle said. "Can't I sleep a little longer? I feel all squared out in the morning."

"You'll feel round soon enough," Pam said. "Now come down here. A good breakfast will get you in shape."

When Danny came downstairs, Bob Circle, his father, was having his breakfast and reading the paper.

"Good morning, son," Bob said through his newspaper. He took a waffle from the plate sitting on the table.

"Those waffles are for Danny," Pam said. "You eat your diet hoops, Bob. Don't take his breakfast."

"I'm hungry!" Bob groaned. "I need real food for breakfast. Something solid, not these empty hoops. They taste like air."

"There, there," Pam said. "You know what Dr. Sphere said. You don't want to get bloated again, dear. You know what happened last time."

Danny was curious. "What *did* happen last time, Dad?"

"Your father's circumference bloated up 5 whole inches," Pam said.

"That's not true," Bob said. "It was just a minor increase. My radius went up by only an inch."

"What about your AREA, Bob?" Pam said. "That shot up like a rocket."

"Area always goes up faster than circumference," Bob said. "That's just the way it is."

1. *If Bob's radius increased by 1 inch, by about how much did his circumference increase?*

   _____

2. *Bob's diet has gotten him down to his old circumference of 25 inches. How big is his radius?*

   _____

3. *By about how many square inches had Bob's area increased when he*

went to see the doctor?

_____

4. *Danny's diameter is normally half of Bob's current diameter. If they both gain half an inch in radius, whose circumference will increase the most? By how much?*

_____

5. *If both Bob and Danny increase their radii by half an inch, whose area will increase more, and by about how much?*

_____

6. *Bob's brother Don Circle is a weightlifter. By training, he increased his radius by one inch last year. The amount he gained in area alone was about the same as Bob's entire area. What is Don's approximate radius?*

_____

"What's in the news, dear?" Pam asked her husband.

"Nothing much," Bob said, looking down at the car ads in his newspaper. "They lowered the price on the new Rectangle-XZ."

"Wow, cool!" Danny said. "Can we get a Rectangle-XZ, Dad? Can we? Huh?"

Bob harumphed. "Now you know we can't afford a new car this year, Dan," Bob said. "If things go well at the Dot Factory, next year we'll get a new Circle-500."

"Bor-r-r-r-ing!" Danny cried.

"Can't we get a Rectangle this time?"

"Don't you understand anything?" Bob said. "We're not SQUARES, we're CIRCLES. We can't get a Rectangle-XZ. We'd never fit inside."

"Why not?" Danny said.

"Well," Bob said, "it's just the way they're made. Those squares—they just fit right in the rectangle-shaped cars. But for us it's different. We don't fit. We get all kinds of gaps."

"But we'd get gaps in a Circle-500, too," Pam said.

"Maybe," Bob said. "But I think the gaps in the Circle-500 would be smaller than the gaps in a Rectangle-XZ."

"I'm not so sure," Pam said.

7. *If Pam's radius is 1 inch greater than Danny's, what is her approximate circumference?*

_____

8. *What would be the dimensions of the smallest Rectangle-XZ the family could buy? (Assume Bob may "bloat up" again to a 5-inch radius, and round Pam's radius to 3.0 and Danny's to 2.0.)*

_____

9. *How much wasted space (in square inches) would it have?*

_____

10. **SUPER CHALLENGE:** *Which has more wasted space: the Rectangle-XZ or the Circle-500?*

_____

DRAW A DIAGRAM/ MAKE A MODEL

Lucy Triangles is having trouble making a triangle with sides that measure 8 inches by 4 inches by 3 inches. Why is this so?

To get a handle on a problem like this use Draw a Diagram. Drawing a diagram lets students really *see* the problem. Relationships in space become clear. So do relationships among numbers.

In this case, have students draw the triangle Lucy is attempting to make, labeling each side, without worrying about proportion or scale.

At first glance, nothing seems wrong. But when they compare the lengths of the sides, students see why the triangle won't "work"—its two short sides are too short!

When they draw the actual triangle, it looks like this:

Clearly, the short side needs to be longer

for this triangle to be a real triangle. But how long does it need to be? Would sides of 8, 4, and 4 form a triangle?

To solve this problem, you might want to have your students make a model out of three thin strips of paper. What advantages do models have over diagrams? They are more real. They can be moved, twisted, and turned around.

Using the model, your students can see that with sides measuring (in inches) 8, 4, and 4 they still come up a little short.

A little common sense says that the sum of the two short sides needs to be *longer* than the long side. Thus, a triangle with sides of 8, 4, and 5 inches will work because the sum of 4 + 5 is greater than 8.

TIPS TO SHARE WITH STUDENTS

When in doubt, use Draw a Diagram. Drawing diagrams helps you visualize almost any kind of problem.

- Label the diagram clearly.

- The diagram you draw need not be a work of art. However, make it clear and keep things in proportion.

- Diagrams work for almost any kind of problem (not just geometrical problems). Sometimes just drawing a picture helps you get a handle on a situation.

- What to do if your diagram doesn't seem to get the job done:

  (**A**) Draw (another) Diagram!

  (**B**) Make a Model.

MODELS: Models are diagrams extended into three-dimensional space. You can make models out of clay, sticks, wood—anything that is convenient. Generally, the guidelines for diagrams apply to models. Keep it simple. Be only as accurate as you need to be. If your model doesn't work—make another model! (Or Draw a Diagram.)

COMBINATIONS: Drawing a diagram works well with most of the other problem-solving strategies, and especially well with:

- Use Easier Numbers

- Guess and Check

CAUTION: Models can be a lot more fun to make than diagrams, but they take more time and effort. Generally speaking, if a diagram will do, use a diagram. Resort to models only when absolutely necessary.

LUCY TRIANGLES

Not much is known about Lucy Tribble's first triangle. Probably she just laid out three sticks, one on top of another and—voila! A triangle!

The rest, as they say, is history. Because from then on, Lucy Tribble became Lucy "Triangles." All day long, from sunup to sundown, she did nothing but plan, think about, and make triangles. "Stop making triangles!" her teachers would say to her. They wrote notes home to her parents.

They sent her to a counselor.
The counselor sent her to a doctor.
The doctor sent her to a specialist.
The specialist sent her to a sub-specialist. The sub-specialist sent her to a sub-sub-specialist, who sent her to a sub-sub-sub specialist, whose specialty, of course, was triangle disorders.

"This is the most triangular child I've ever seen in my life," the sub-sub-sub-specialist finally said.

Lucy's parents cringed. "Is it something to worry about?" they asked.

"No," the specialist said. "It's wonderful!"

From there, there was only one place that Lucy could go: the prestigious Triangle Institute in Twitzerland.

And it was in Twitzerland that Lucy did her best work. She invented new triangles and improved on old ones. Invisible triangles...circular triangles...four-sided triangles... cornerless triangles...reversible triangles...inside-out triangles...liquid triangles....These were the great triangular problems of the day, and Lucy solved them all.

In fact, she never met a triangle problem she didn't like—until the Twiss president, Jean-Louis LaCheese, asked for submissions for the Tricentennial Triangle, honoring 300 years of the Twiss Republic. LaCheese's idea was that the Tricentennial Triangle would have sides of 100 inches by 66 inches by 33 inches; 100 for the number of stars, 66 for stripes, and 33 for the number of goats on the Twiss flag.

For three days the entire Twiss Republic waited breathlessly for Lucy to present her design. Finally, she came to the Presidential Palace, and gave the President her design. The President unrolled the scroll. "Why this is empty!" he cried. "What is the meaning of this?"

1. ***Can you explain the meaning of Lucy's "failure" to come up with a design?***

   _____

   _____

   _____

Lucy spoke plainly to President LaCheese. She could not design the triangle until he agreed to change the lengths of its sides. Reluctantly, the President agreed. Lucy could increase the length of one side, and one side only.

2. ***Which side should she choose—the stars side, stripes side, or goats side?***

   _____

Then President LaCheese added that if Lucy *increased* the length of one side,

she would need to *decrease* the length of another side by the same amount.

3. ***Which sides should increase and decrease? By how much?***

   _____

4. ***From Problem 3, which two sides cannot be increased and decreased by the same amount?***

   _____

Suppose Lucy decreases the number of stars by 1 to 99 without changing the other two quantities.

5. ***What will her "triangle" look like?***

   _____

6. ***President LaCheese gave Lucy another option. She could double the length of the any of the three sides. Which side should Lucy double in length?***

   _____

7. ***LaCheese prefers skinny triangles to fat ones. How does this change your answer to Question 6?***

   _____

8. ***Suppose Lucy could triple the length of the any of the three sides. Which side should she triple?***

   _____

SHA LING AND THE THREE WISHES

There was a girl named Sha Ling who wasn't at all greedy until she found a magic lamp and rubbed it. Out came a genie with a turban on his head and rings in his ears.

"You have 3 wishes," the genie said.

"I've heard this one before," Sha Ling said. "Forget it. You're going to trick me into wasting my wishes. No thanks."

"But sire—" the genie cried.

"Don't 'sire' me," Sha said. "I'm not your sire. I'm a girl and my name is Sha Ling and maybe I'm not even interested in your silly old wishes."

The genie started to cry.

"Oh, all right," Sha Ling said. "If you want me to wish, I'll wish. Just stop blubbering."

For her first wish Sha Ling wished for 3 new wishes.

"This is highly irregular, sire," the genie cried. Nevertheless, Sha was granted her wish.

1. *How many of her original 3 wishes does Sha have left?*

_____

2. *How many wishes does Sha have in all?*

_____

For her second and third wishes Sha also wished for 3 more wishes. The genie frowned, but granted them.

3. *How many of her original 3 wishes does Sha have left?*

_____

4. *How many new wishes does Sha have now?*

_____

Now Sha remarked, "You're not looking well, genie. What's wrong?" She knew only too well. The genie was afraid she would use each of her new wishes to wish for 3 even newer wishes. Which was exactly what she did.

5. *How many new wishes does Sha have now?*

_____

Now the genie knew he was in real trouble. If Sha kept wishing for new wishes he would be ruined. So he decided to propose a deal. "This is my best offer," he said to Sha. "I'll grant you ONE last wish—but only one. With your wish you may wish for ONE HUNDRED new wishes, instead of three. Surely, that should be enough, sire."

6. *Should Sha take the genie's deal? Why or why not?*

_____

_____

_____

Sha didn't take the offer. Instead, she just wished and wished and wished. She wished so much that her mouth got rubbery from saying the word "WISH" so much. She wished so much that her wishbone began to ache.

But still, she kept on wishing. She used up all her new wishes from before, got more new wishes, and then used those to get even more new wishes.

Now Sha had a total of 240 wishes, and she was feeling pretty pleased with herself. But this time it was the genie's turn to laugh.

"You may have a lot of wishes," he said, "but I forgot to tell you one thing: YOU MUST USE UP ALL YOUR WISHES BY SUNDOWN OR YOU LOSE THEM ALL!"

Sha sighed. In 15 minutes it would be sundown. How could she possibly use up all those wishes? Suddenly she had an idea. She would use up 3 wishes to wish her friends Ting, Ping, and Shwee Ta were with her. Together, they would use up all the wishes. And that's exactly what they did!

7. *On the average, about how many wishes would Sha and each of her friends need to make each minute to use up all of Sha's wishes?*

_____

THE LEAKY TOP CORPORATION

LOUIE: Hello? Leaky Top Corporation. If you have the bottom, we have a LEAKY TOP for it. This is Leaky Louie speaking. How can I help you?

CALLER: Hi, Leaky Louie. Listen. I've got a can, a simple soft-drink-shaped can, with a circular opening, and I'd like a leaky top for it. Can you help me out?

LOUIE: Can we help you out! Are you kidding? We've got HUNDREDS of different leaky tops for that can of yours. What would you like? Something in a triangle, perhaps? Right now, we're running a big sale on equiangular—

CALLER: I'd like something simple, Louie. Just a simple top that leaks.

LOUIE: Would you like the top to leak through holes in the middle or out the sides?

CALLER: Gee, I don't know. Out the sides, I guess.

LOUIE: And a very wise choice indeed, ma'am. Now, for the shape, I assume you'll be wanting something in a regular polygon.

CALLER: A regular polygon?

LOUIE: You know—a shape in which all the sides and interior angles are equal.

CALLER: That sounds fine. Is it expensive?

LOUIE: Prices are based only on how leaky the top you choose is. The more it leaks, the more you pay. Now, what size circle are we talking about?

CALLER: Why do you need to know that?

LOUIE: Let me explain something here, ma'am. Our tops may leak, but they FIT PERFECTLY. Each top reaches precisely across the container's opening, leaking precisely where it's supposed to leak.

CALLER: Oh, I didn't know that. This can's 6 inches in diameter. I measured it myself.

LOUIE: Great. Now let's see what we can do for you.

1. *Which shape would leak more, a square or an equilateral triangle?*

   _____

2. *Which shape would have more gaps, the triangle or the square?*

   _____

3. *Which shape would have larger gaps, the triangle or the square?*

   _____

4. *Which shape would be more expensive, a regular pentagon or a regular hexagon?*

   _____

5. *Which gaps would be larger—those formed by a regular 8-sided or a regular 12-sided figure?*

   _____

6. *Suppose the caller put marbles with diameters of 1 inch in the can. Would they leak out of the can with a square top? Why or why not?*

   _____

   _____

   _____

7. *Would marbles with 1/2 inch diameters leak out? Why or why not?*

   _____

   _____

   _____

8. **SUPER CHALLENGE:** *Suppose you could add up all the gaps for a can with square top and arrange them as one large, round hole. About how big a marble (in diameter) would fit through them?*

   _____

GHENGIS IN LOVE

Out of plastic, wire,
Metal and sand
Dr. Rona Beale
Made an artificial man
    She named him Ghengis....

Ghengis was so life-like
And real
That he fell in love
With Dr. Beale
    He had it bad....

And not just love,
But head over heels
Knocked off his feet
You know how it feels
    He had it real bad....

He sent her artificial poems
And artificial ballads
His artificial love
Was absolutely valid
    Or so he claimed....

He followed her around in an
Artificial swoon
She said "This must stop,
And it better stop soon,"
    But it didn't....

So late one night
She took her prized creation
Opened up his brain and performed an
operation
    A "brain-ectomy"....

The next morning she heard
A knock at her door
"Dr. Beale," Ghengis said,

"I don't love you anymore."
    "Great," she said....

Which was better than great
For now she was free
To give speeches, win awards
And appear on TV
    With Ghengis....

And everywhere she went
She took him along
He seemed so real
But something was wrong
    With Ghengis....

There was a sadness in him
She could not deny
To pretend it wasn't there
Would be telling a lie
    So she worried....

As time passed
The sadness grew
Until finally there was only
One thing left to do
    So she did it....

She said, "I may be crazy,
I may be insane,
But I'm going to give you
Back your old brain,"
        So she gave it....

The operation took all night
She finished at dawn
And when she finished
The sadness was gone
        Just vanished....

Ghengis looked at her, and laughed
And then—
He knew that he
Was in love again
        He had it bad....

He felt so happy
He thought he would cry
He just had one question
And that question was "Why?"
        Why did she do it?...

After all that trouble
And all that pain
Why would she give him
Back his old brain?
        He wondered....

"Did you ever consider,
That I'm the one who
Could have fallen head over heels
In love with you?"
        She asked him....

Not to get mushy, or gooey
Or sappy
From that day forward, they
Were blissfully,
        absolutely,
                artificially happy.

Ghengis's box-shaped brain pan measured 2 by 2 by 2 1/2 feet. Dr. Steele created the brain units below. They came in two sizes as shown.

EMPTY BRAIN PAN

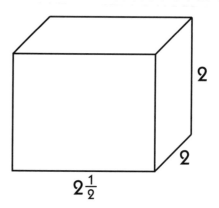

BIG UNITS

TRUTH,
BEAUTY,
LOVE,
LOGIC,
LAUGHTER

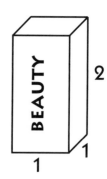

SMALL UNITS

HAPPINESS,
LONELINESS,
COMPASSION,
SADNESS,
JEALOUSY,
ANGER,
CONTENTMENT,
HATE, FEAR, JUSTICE

1. *Is there enough room in Ghengis's brain pan for all the units?*

   _____

2. *If there were an unlimited supply of big units, how many could fit into the brain pan?*

   _____

3. *If there were an unlimited supply of small units, how many would fit in brain pan?*

   _____

4. *If as many large units as possible are included, how many large and small brain units would fit in*

Ghengis's brain pan?

   _____

5. *Show how you would arrange the units in your answer to Problem 3.*

   _____

   _____

   _____

6. **SUPER CHALLENGE:** *Design a box that would hold all 15 units, big and small. How much leftover space is in your box?*

   _____

THE DOGFINDERS

My name's Doc Dachshund. This is my partner, Carol Spaniel. You lose your dog—we'll find it. We're the DogFinders. Call us at 1-800-FIND-DOG.

Today I want to tell you about Case 503-B. Otherwise known as "Snarfy." Carol and I are sitting in the main office, chewing on a bone. The phone rings. Carol picks it up. It's a guy named Shnowzer. He has sort of a "barky" voice. And he's talking a mile a minute about a lost dog.

"Slow down," Carol says. "What's the dog's name?"

"Snarfy," the guy says. "Snarfy Shnowzer."

"Looks like a job for the BOW-WOW," I say.

BOW-WOW stands for the Bark Or Woof - Whimper Or Whine Dog Detector. It's a machine that electronically detects the barks, woofs, whines, and whimpers of a lost dog.

We turn it on and start getting a reading, which consists of two numbers. The first is either north or south. The second is either east or west. For example, if we get a reading of 3-2 it means the dog is 3 blocks north or south of us, and 2 blocks east or west.

For Snarfy we get a reading of 4-6. It really seems like an open-and-shut case.

1. *How many possible locations are there for Snarfy right now?*

_____

2. *The next reading we get is 8-6. Did Snarfy get closer or farther away from BOW-WOW?*

_____

3. *Then we get a reading of 6-8. Did Snarfy move? If so, did he get closer or farther away from BOW-WOW?*

_____

We wait for Snarfy to stay in the same place for awhile. He seems to fall asleep at 6-8. Then Carol makes her move. She takes the mobile BOW-WOW unit 3 blocks due south of the main office. The reading changes from 6-8 to 3-8.

Back at the main office, I'm still getting a reading of 6-8. When Carol returns we compare notes.

4. **What does Carol's reading tell you about Snarfy's location?**

_____

_____

5. **How many possible locations are there for Snarfy now?**

_____

Next, Carol goes 3 blocks due east of the main office with the mobile BOW-WOW and gets a reading of 6-11. I've still got a reading of 6-8 on the main unit.

6. **Where is Snarfy?**

_____

_____

7. **If Carol had gone 3 blocks west instead of east to get her second reading, what would the reading have been?**

_____

So now that we know the exact location of the dog we put on our protective uniforms and load up our gravy guns. Our guns shoot gravy-flavored dog biscuits. We use them to lure the dogs toward us.

We come to the corner of 6th Avenue and 8th Street. This has to be the place. We shoot a few warning shots. A little snipper dog comes running over and grabs them up. Sure enough, it's Snarfy. His name is on his collar.

So Carol and I take Snarfy back to the main office. Then I call up Mr. Schnowzer.

"We've found Snarfy," I tell him. "You can come on down and pick him up."

When Mr. Schnowzer shows up, he and Snarfy are so glad to see each other that they start jumping up and down and yapping away. When the racket finally dies down, Mr. Schnowzer turns to me and barks, "Thanks so much. And by the way. How much do I owe you?"

"Well let's see," I start calculating. "It was a standard dog finding job. About 20 minutes on the Mobile BOW-WOW unit. It's going to run you a full biscuit."

"Can I write you a check?" asks Mr. Schnowzer.

"Sure," I say.

But the next day I go into the bank to cash Mr. Schnowzer's check. And wouldn't you know it, the check bounces. I guess that's what you call a rubber biscuit.

YOUR TURN

Make up your own problem using the BOW-WOW Dog-Detector.

ROMANCE FOOTBALL

PHIL: Welcome to Romance Football, the only game in the world that combines the heartbreak of romance, and the bone-bruising excitement of professional football. I'm your host, Phil O'Steen.

LINDA: And I'm Linda Lipps. As you know, Phil, Romance Football is played on a full-sized football field. And now, here come our players.

PHIL: Daphne and Rob line up on Rob's 25-yard line. Rob asks the crowd of over 73,000 for quiet. Here's the play: Daphne comes on fast, telling Rob she wants to break up. Rob is stunned. "What do you mean?" he says. Daphne says they never have any real fun anymore, anyway. Rob is down! He's down on his own 30-yard line!

LINDA: Now he's up. Rob asks her if there is someone else. Daphne denies it. "What about Steve?" Rob asks. Ooh, this is exciting! "Steve's just a friend," she says. "Oh yeah?" Rob says. "Then why is he standing over there?"

And there Steve is, Phil, down on Daphne's goal line! Rob's making a break for him. He's in the clear. The thirty, the forty, the fifty....

1. *Assuming that Rob starts running on the 30-yard line, how many seconds will it take him to reach Daphne's goal line if he runs at a speed of 10 yards per second?*

_____

2. *Assuming that Rob and Daphne run at the same speed, if Rob gets a half-second jump on Daphne, how far ahead of her will he remain as he runs downfield?*

_____

3. *If Daphne slips on Rob's 45-yard line and is down for 1 second, where will Rob be when she starts running again? How about if she's down for 2 1/2 seconds?*

_____

_____

4. *If Steve runs toward Rob at 10 yards per second, where will the two meet?*

_____

5. *How long will it take Steve and Rob to meet?*

_____

6. **SUPER CHALLENGE:** *On another play, Rob and Daphne are on the 50-yard line. Steve is on the goal line 50 yards away from Rob, directly across the field. Daphne is not directly across from Steve, because she is standing on the 50-yard line 20 yards away from Rob. How far is Daphne from Steve?*

_____

LINDA: Rob has met up with Steve now, Phil. He looks upset. Steve is trying to explain something to him. Ooh, here comes Daphne. "Steve never meant anything to me," she claims.

PHIL: Now Steve looks hurt. He's woozy, Linda. This is unbelievable—what a turnaround! Daphne's trying to explain something to Steve. She takes his hand. Wait! Now Rob seems to be in distress again. But what's this? Is Steve moving in for a kiss? Is this unbelievable or what, Linda?

LINDA: Unbelievable, Phil. At first I thought Rob was going to get angry again. But now he just looks sad. He's a beaten man. Ooh, this is ugly. I never thought I'd see the day when Rob Rothman got taken out by a little unromantic peck on the cheek like that. But wait! What's this?

PHIL: It's the old sucker play, Linda. That kiss we just saw—it was a fake! Steve is really Daphne's cousin! And the two of them were just trying to make Rob jealous. Unbelievable!

LINDA: Well, now I've seen everything, Phil. What a play! Now Rob's moving in. Daphne comes to him. They're making up, Phil! It's going to be a reverse side pucker kiss with a 2.9 degree of difficulty. Oh, I hope these two can pull it off...

PHIL: They're into the squeeze now, Linda. Would you look at Daphne's eyelids fluttering. And there! Rob's famous Lip Tremble! What a perfect move, Linda. Now they're going for it all—the look, the squeeze, the pucker—TOUCHDOWN! A perfect 3-point side-pucker landing, Linda! Wow! Can you believe how soft that was?

LINDA: All I can say, Phil, is, ain't love grand?

LOST ON NOWHERE

"**I** told you not to push GO," Lupe said.

"Yes you did," Joe said. "You said 'GO JOE.'"

"I said 'NO JOE,' not 'GO JOE,'" Lupe said.

"Oh," Joe said. "Well, whatever. Here we are."

They looked outside of their spaceship at the barren asteroid.

"Looks like we missed the moon," Joe said.

"Yeah," Lupe said.

"And Mars, too," Joe said. "And Venus. And Neptune. And Jupiter. And Jupiter's moons. And...."

"Okay, okay," Lupe said. "I get the picture. You don't need to rub it in."

"I'm not rubbing it in," Joe said. "My father told me not to trust a spaceship that was created in someone's garage."

"It was *your* garage," Lupe said.

"Yeah, but it was *your* idea," Joe said. "Remember. I wanted to build a car. But you wanted a spaceship. Hey, I need to stretch my legs. I'm gonna stop."

Joe and Lupe landed on the asteroid. "I wonder what they call this place?" Joe asked.

"How about Nowhere," Lupe said.

"Well, let's get out and have a look around," Joe said. "The sooner we get some measurements made, the sooner

we can turn around and go back home."

The first thing Lupe and Joe needed to know was how big Nowhere was. To do this, they separated. Lupe waited until the sun reached its highest point in the sky—high noon. Six miles away, Joe noticed that at his location the sun didn't reach "high noon" until an hour and a half had passed.

"I think our calculations are correct," Joe said, "but we'll need to wait until 'high noon' tomorrow so we can check our readings."

1. *What would the distance around Nowhere be if it had a 24-hour day?*

_____

2. *The next day, Lupe and Joe realized that Nowhere had a 20-hour day instead of a 24-hour day. Will this increase, decrease, or have no effect on their measurement of the asteroid's circumference?*

_____

3. *Assuming that the asteroid spins on its axis once in a 20-hour day, calculate the speed at which it spins.*

_____

4. *The circumference of Earth is about 25,000 miles at the equator. (A) How fast does the Earth spin, in miles per hour, to the nearest thousand? (B) About how many times faster or slower does Earth spin than Nowhere?*

_____

"Did you hear that?" Joe said.

"What?" Lupe said.

"That bubbling," Joe said. Now Lupe heard it too.

"Must be volcanic activity," she said. Suddenly, something squirted up out of the ground.

"Oh my gosh!" Lupe cried.

"What? What is it?" Joe asked.

Lupe tasted the molten green liquid.

"Well, I could be mistaken," she said, "but to me it looks, tastes, and smells like cheese. In fact, I'm sure of it. It is cheese. Green cheese."

"You mean *cheese*, the stuff you make sandwiches with?" Joe asked. He tasted the substance himself. "Oh my gosh," he said. "It *is* cheese."

"Are you thinking what I'm thinking?" Lupe asked.

"We could corner the world market on cheese sandwiches," Joe said.

"We're rich!" Lupe cried. The

cheese was still gushing out of the hole.

5. *While going over their calculations, Lupe and Joe found out that their figure for the distance around the asteroid was correct, but the shape was wrong. The asteroid was cube-shaped, a perfect cube. What is the distance across each face of the cube?*

_____

6. *Assuming the cube-shaped asteroid is hollow and filled with cheese, how many cubic miles of cheese are inside?*

_____

"Wow, that's a lot of cheese," Joe said.

"Can you imagine what this could mean back on Earth?" Lupe said.

"What?"

"Cheese prices would plummet," Lupe said. "And along with that, everything else. The cheese on this asteroid could cause a world-wide depression."

"Wow," Joe said. "I never thought of it that way. Maybe we just better close up this hole and go back to where we came from."

"You're right," Lupe said. "Let's go."

And so they zoomed off into space, until the asteroid, and its cheese, were just a tiny speck in the distance.

MAKE A TABLE/ ORGANIZE A LIST

Gwynn has a problem: she has a clock that loses 15 minutes every hour. If it reads the correct time at 12 noon, what time will it read when the actual time is 6 o'clock in the evening?

Problems like this can get extremely confusing. To keep everything straight, it's a good idea for students to use Make a Table. The table at right shows both the real time and the time on Gwynn's clock.

REAL TIME	GWYNN'S TIME
12 Noon	12 Noon
1:00 PM	12:45 PM
2:00 PM	1:30 PM
3:00 PM	2:15 PM
4:00 PM	3:00 PM
5:00 PM	3:45 PM
6:00 PM	4:30 PM

Making the table does more than tell students that Gwynn's clock will read 4:30 when it is really 6 o'clock. It allows them to see a pattern. To see this pattern more clearly, extend the diagram.

REAL TIME	GWYNN'S TIME
7:00 PM	5:15 PM
8:00 PM	6:00 PM
9:00 PM	6:45 PM
10:00 PM	7:30 PM
11:00 PM	8:15 PM
12 Midnight	9:00 PM
1:00 AM	9:45 PM

Now they can see that Gwynn's clock loses a full hour for every 4 hours that pass. It is 1 hour slow after 4 hours, 2 hours slow after 8 hours, 3 hours slow after 12 hours, and so on. Recognizing the pattern allows your students to answer questions like this one:

What time will Gwynn's clock read after 24 hours have passed?

To solve this problem, we simplified the table somewhat. From this table it is clear that Gwynn's clock will be 6 hours behind at 12 noon on the following day, reading 6 o'clock in the morning.

REAL TIME	GWYNN'S TIME	HOURS BEHIND
12 Noon	12 Noon	0
4:00 PM	3:00 PM	1
8:00 PM	6:00 PM	2
12 Midnight	9:00 PM	3
4:00 AM	12:00 PM	4
8:00 AM	3:00 AM	5
12 Noon	6:00 AM	6

TIPS TO SHARE WITH STUDENTS

- Use Make a Table to organize data or keep track of confusing numbers and facts.

- Use Make a Table to spot trends and identify patterns.

- Use Make a Table to identify patterns or correlate one set of facts to another.

- Keep tables simple, if possible. List only the information you need.

COMBINATIONS: Making a table works well with most of the other problem-solving strategies, and especially well with:

- Draw a Diagram
- Work Backwards

A THOUSAND CLOCKS

Gwynn was always wasting time fooling around with things and she was never PUNCTUAL, which drove her mother bonkers but didn't bother Gwynn a bit.

One day after school she was out messing around with something—maybe it was a broken radio, or maybe it wasn't. Suddenly, she realized that it was a clock, an incredibly broken clock, all gummed-up and rusted with its springs sprung and its hands bent like pretzels.

On the back was an incredibly filthy and smudged sticker that read: *GUARANTEED FOR LIFE OR YOUR MONEY BACK—THE OFF-TIME CLOCK COMPANY.*

The Off-Time Clock Company? It sounded like a joke. But it was the kind of joke Gwynn liked, so she put on her torn jacket and hopped on her squeaky bicycle with the broken gears and pedaled down several narrow, twisting streets in the dark part of town until she reached the Off-Time Clock Company.

She went inside and was immediately assaulted by the tickings, tockings, clickings, clockings, cuckooings, and whirrings of what seemed to be a thousand clocks, every one reading a different time.

"Can I help you?" a man asked her. "I'm Reggie."

Gwynn put her incredibly broken, rusted, and pretzeled-up clock on the counter.

"This thing doesn't work," she said.

"How do you know?" Reggie asked.

"Look," Gwynn said. "It's early afternoon. This clock says 9:35. It's goofier than a three-dollar bill. I want my money back."

"Maybe you don't understand," Reggie said. "My clocks are guaranteed to tell the WRONG time, not the right time."

This threw Gwynn for a loop. Who would want a clock or a watch that told the wrong time?

"Lots of people," Reggie said.

"Like who?" Gwynn demanded.

"Well," Reggie said, "suppose you're someone who likes to live in the past. Or suppose you're late all the time but you'd rather be early. Or early all the time and you'd rather be late."

"Speaking of being late," Gwynn

said, "you got the time? I'm supposed to be home at 5:15."

Reggie pointed to the thousand clocks in the room all ticking away like mad. "Take your pick," he said.

(Assume that at exactly 12 o'clock all clocks are set to read the correct time.)

1. *Reggie showed Gwynn a clock that gained a half-hour of time every hour. How long would it take for it to read the right time?*

_____

2. *How long would it take for a clock that lost a half-hour of time every hour to read the right time?*

_____

3. *How long would it take for a clock that gained 10 minutes every hour to read the right time?*

_____

4. *For a clock that lost 10 minutes every hour, would your answer be greater than your answer for Problem 3, less, or the same?*

_____

5. *Will your answer to Problem 3 increase or decrease for a clock that gains 5 minutes an hour?*

_____

_____

6. *How could you design a clock that would almost never be correct?*

_____

_____

_____

_____

The Off-Time Clock Company was definitely Gwynn's kind of store. She was so impressed that she decided to buy something from Reggie. Gwynn chose a watch—a see-through, glow-in-the-dark model with tiny crooked hands.

"Now I'm going to set this watch against our master clock," said Reggie. "It is now exactly 4:15. And from this point forward it's guaranteed to lose 12 minutes an hour."

But a strange thing happened as Gwynn was riding home. She was pedaling along when suddenly she spotted some broken, stained, and otherwise useless thing on the side of the road. This was the perfect kind of item to waste the whole afternoon on, messing around.

But somehow, Gwynn didn't feel like messing around.

And in fact, when she looked down at her see-through, glow-in-the-dark, guaranteed-to-lose-12-minutes-an-hour watch, Gwynn started to wonder.

And the more she wondered, the more confused she got.

"Let's see," she thought to herself. "If it was exactly 4:15 when I left the shop and my watch says it's now 4:39 that means it's really 4:15 plus the 24 minutes minus the 12 minutes lost except it wouldn't really be 12 yet because...."

And the more confused she got, the more curious she became about what the time really was.

And the more curious she became, the more she realized that there was only one way to find out: Go home.

Which is exactly what she did, almost giving her mother HEART FAILURE, because it was the first time Gwynn had been PUNCTUAL in so long that her mother couldn't even remember.

"What are you doing here?" her mother asked. "You're not even late."

"I'm sorry," Gwynn said.

"Don't be sorry," her mother said. "Just tell me what happened."

So Gwynn showed her the watch, and told her about Reggie and the Off-Time Clock Company. And from that day on Gwynn never went anywhere without that watch. And because the watch was (almost) never correct, Gwynn never stopped wondering what the time really was.

The upshot was that she started coming home ON TIME and sometimes even EARLY. Which wasn't actually a CONTRADICTION because she never had anything against being PUNCTUAL in the first place, it was always just that she was messing around with something, and wasn't paying any attention.

But her mother thought it was the greatest thing since sliced bread.

"Do you know what this means?" she asked her daughter.

"Does it mean that you're not going to go bonkers from me being late all the time?" Gwynn said.

Gwynn's mother beamed. "Exactly," she said.

And the two of them lived happily ever after. More or less.

7. *What time was it really when Gwynn's watch said 4:39?*

_____

THE FOUR TOOTHBRUSHES

It was a bad time to be a toothbrush bird.

Ted and Wally were both toothbrushes. They worked for the crocodiles, pecking out scraps from between their teeth.

But lately the crocodiles were talking about giving up their old evil ways and becoming vegetarians.

"It's a trick," Wally said. "The crocs don't really like cereal. They're just sandbagging."

"Maybe so," Ted said. "But in the meantime, what do we toothbrushes do?"

"We'll sing," Wally said.

"But we don't know how to sing," Ted said.

"We're birds," Wally said. "All birds know how to sing. Listen—"

So Wally sang: "Doo wop doo doo wop doo doo wop doo doo!"

Suddenly, Ted had an uncontrollable urge to join in: "Dooba dooba dooba dooba dooba dobba doo!"

And Wally came back with: "Shee bop badee bop bobba bobba bobba bobba bobba bob bob bob bob ba-dop!"

And the Four Toothbrushes were born. (Actually, the other two Toothbrushes, Bill and Eddy, joined up later.)

They played all the big clubs. From the beginning, they had their own sound, and everyone loved it.

"You guys are fantastic!" Jerry Dee crowed. Jerry was a top talent agent who represented all the top bird acts, including Billie Nightingale and the Bluebirds. He had a greedy smile and smoked a green cigar.

"I'm going to make you boys famous," Jerry said.

"We already are famous," Ted said.

"That's what you think," Jerry Dee. said. And he pulled a long contract out of his briefcase.

1. *Jerry offered the Toothbrushes Deal A: They are to receive $10,000 cash and 10 percent of sales for every CD over 10,000 that was sold. How much would the Toothbrushes make on this deal if they sold 20,000 CD's for $10 each?*

_____

2. *How much would they make on the deal if they sold 9,000 CD's?*

_____

3. *Deal B would give the Toothbrushes $20,000 cash and 10 percent of sales for every CD over 20,000 that was sold. How much would they make if they sold 30,000 CD's?*

_____

4. *Which deal would you advise the Toothbrushes to take? Explain your answer:*

_____

_____

_____

_____

5. *How much would Deal A pay if the Toothbrushes sold 100,000 CD's? 439,000 CD's?*

_____

6. *How much money do the Toothbrushes earn per CD no matter how many they sell?*

_____

Jerry made good on his promise. Before much time passed, the Four Toothbrushes were famous. They got so famous they didn't know up from down.

But, being famous, like most things, had its sad side. Ted was lonely and he missed the jungle.

"I wonder what the crocodiles are doing now," he said.

"Oh, who cares about the crocodiles," Wally said.

"To tell you the truth, I do," Ted said. "The food here is good, but nothing's as good as the food we got from the crocodiles."

"You're right," Wally admitted.

It would be nice to report that at that very moment they flew straight off to the jungle, found the crocodiles, and never came back again.

But they didn't because they were too rich and famous. And because they had to go on a fifty-city concert tour. So instead, they hired some meat-eating crocodiles to go on the road with them. After that, the Four Toothbrushes feasted on a delicious "jungle breakfast" each and every morning in their lavish hotel suite. Just like the old days (sort of).

BIRTHA BIXTON AND HER BELOVED PURPLE CALCULATOR

Twelve-year-old Birtha Bixton loved to compute. As the neighborhood kids amused themselves playing four-square or Barbies, Birtha would sit in her room and with the aid of her beloved purple calculator, wile away the hours figuring out the square root of the total number of flowers on her wallpaper or what thirty-five percent of all the people in Detroit plus Iceland amounted to. She was known to be very meticulous and to possess a finger with an inch-tall callous—the result of all that button pushing. When asked what she did with the answers to all of those bizarre math questions, she merely pointed to a huge gray cabinet and said: "I file them."

On April Fool's Day, Birtha's brother, Barney, decided the time was ripe to play a trick on his "calculating" sister. So when Birtha was out walking her poodle named Abacus, Barney—a computer programing buff—sneaked into her room. There, he took apart her beloved purple calculator and tinkered with its intricate workings. "This will add some spice to her calculations," he snickered.

After walking Abacus, Birtha returned to her room, refreshed and ready to embark on her most challenging project to date: adding up all the digits of every phone number in the Pinkney County phone book. She cracked her knuckles, turned on her calculator, and opened the phone book to the first name and number: Ababa, Abby — 924-3218. To add the digits, she pushed 9 + 2 + 4 + 3 + 2 + 1 + 8, then =, and got an answer of 37. But 37 didn't seem quite right so she added the numbers again in her head and, just as she suspected, got a different answer: 29. "What's going on here!" she exclaimed.

Then she heard it—Barney's chortle on the other side of her door—and quickly put two and two together.

"O.K. Barney," she said, opening the door, "the jig is up. What did you do to my calculator?"

"Well," responded Barney with a devious grin, "in honor of April Fool's Day, I rigged it so that each button you push represents a number different from itself."

"Very sneaky," said Birtha (who always relished a challenge). "I'll just have to figure out which number's which."

"In that case, I'll provide you with a few clues," said Barney.

CLUE A: The button marked 1 really equals 3.

CLUE B: When added together on the purple calculator, the digits of the phone number 211-2211 equal 36.

1. *What number does the 2 button really represent?*

_____

CLUE C: When added together on the purple calculator, the digits of the phone number 321-3122 equal 30.

2. *What number does the 3 button really represent?*

_____

CLUE D: When added together on the purple calculator, the digits of the phone number 434-1122 equal 32.

3. *What number does the 4 button really represent?*

_____

CLUE E: When added together on the purple calculator, the digits of the phone number 554-1234 equal 39.

4. *What number does the 5 button really represent?*

_____

CLUE F: When added together on the purple calculator, the digits of the phone number 612-4355 equal 38.

5. *What number does the 6 button really represent?*

_____

CLUE G: When added together on the purple calculator, the digits of the phone number 767-5314 equal 23.

6. *What number does the 7 button really represent?*

_____

CLUE H: When added together on the purple calculator, the digits of the phone number 815-4237 equal 33.

7. *What number does the 8 button really represent?*

_____

CLUE I: When added together on the purple calculator, the digits of the phone number 924-3218 equal 37.

8. *What number does the 9 button really represent?*

_____

CLUE J: When added together on the purple calculator, the digits of the phone number 204-8933 equal 28.

9. ***What number does the 0 button really represent?***

_____

EPILOGUE

With the aid of Barney's clues, Birtha figured out which number was which faster than you can say "Pythagorean theorem." Later, when Barney offered to reprogram the calculator so that the buttons would represent the correct numbers, Birtha said, "Don't bother."

"Why not?" asked Barney.

"The mixed-up numbers make calculating all the more invigorating," responded Birtha.

"Sis, you take the cake," said Barney, exiting her room.

But Birtha didn't care a digit what he thought. She was happy to be alone, once again, with her beloved purple calculator.

THE MONDAY BLUES

The **Student Council at** Baxter School was in a bad mood. They were tired of passing laws and voting on issues that nobody cared about. This time they were going to do something that made a difference.

"What should we do?" Council President Molly Green asked.

"Let's increase recess to two hours!" someone suggested.

"Yeah! Yeah!" everyone laughed.

Molly rapped with her gavel. "Order!" she barked. "Any other suggestions?"

"Let's ban homework," someone else said.

Everyone laughed again, including Molly. "We don't really have the power to ban homework," she said. "But I do like the idea of banning something. What else could we ban?"

They tried several ideas until they finally hit upon the perfect thing: No one liked it. No one needed it. And no one would ever miss it when it was gone:

Monday.

"Can we really ban Mondays?" someone asked Molly.

"Why not?" Molly said. "This is a democracy, isn't it? We can ban anything we like."

So from that day forward, Mondays just didn't exist at Baxter School. The school week started on a Tuesday, then went to Wednesday, Thursday, Friday, Saturday, Sunday, then back to Tuesday again.

Which was great, except for what it did to the calendar. So they made two calendars. One was the "Baxter Calendar" that had no Mondays. The other was the "real" calendar that the rest of the world used.

They started their system on Monday, December 1. Of course, they changed this date to Tuesday, December 1.

1. *How many days are in a Baxter Calendar week?*

_____

2. *On the real calendar, on what day of the week did December 9th fall? On the Baxter Calendar, what day of the week was the 9th of December?*

_____

3. *On the Baxter Calendar, on what day of the week did New Year's Day fall?*

_____

4. *By how many days did New Year's come late or early for Baxter school?*

_____

On February 1st, the Council met to decide if the "Baxter Calendar" would continue. Some council members were against it. What did it do besides confuse everyone?

"I'll tell you what it did," said a voice from the back. "It gave us more weekends and less weekdays."

5. *Did the Baxter Calendar really provide more weekend days? If so, how many more weekend days during December and January did it provide?*

_____

6. *Were there really fewer weekdays in December and January with the Baxter Calendar? How many fewer?*

_____

7. **SUPER CHALLENGE:** *Molly stood up and reminded everyone that by state law the school year needed to have 180 school days in it. Estimate what this would mean for summer vacation. Would it come sooner or later than normal? About how much sooner or later?*

_____

YOUR TURN
• • • • • • • • • •

Make up your own problem using the calendar. You can use the "Baxter Calendar" or make up one of your own.

THE CRYSTAL BEAN-POT LOTTERY

Chap and Fiona worked in the same office at City Hall. Not a day passed by when Chap didn't come up with some plan to impress the Mayor.

"What about a lottery?" Chap suggested. "That would raise a lot of money for the city."

"What kind of lottery?" Fiona asked.

"A Crystal Bean-Pot lottery," Chap said. "Put 10,000 beans in a pot. Only 50 are Crystal Beans. The rest are Ordinary Beans. People pay 1 dollar to pick a bean out of the pot. If it's an ordinary bean, they throw it away. If it's a crystal bean, they win $100 and they put the bean back in the pot."

"What a ridiculous plan," Fiona said. "It's a good thing the Mayor never looks at suggestions from lowly workers like us, because if he did, he would laugh his head off."

But in fact the Mayor did look at the suggestion. Some time later they received a call.

"Our idea! Our idea!" Fiona cried. "They're going to use our idea. Can you believe it, Chap?"

"What do you mean, *our* idea?" Chap said. "It was *my* idea. You said it was a ridiculous idea!"

"That was before the Mayor called," Fiona said.

Soon after that, the Crystal Bean-Pot Lottery officially began. Chap and Fiona were put in charge of it.

After one week of operation more than 500 people took beans from the pot and only TWO were winners. "That's fantastic!" Fiona cried. "Think of the profit we're making!"

Over the next few weeks, the results were similar. Then, after about three months, the number of winners started to increase. One week there were 5 winners. Then 7. After 4 months (16 weeks) the number of winners jumped to 10. Week 17 had 12 winners. Week 18 had 17 winners. It didn't make any sense because the same number of people—about 500—

played the game every week.

Why were there so many more winners?

"I can't understand it," Chap said.

Suddenly the phone rang. Fiona answered. It was the Mayor's office. The Mayor wanted an explanation for what was going wrong with the lottery.

"You're in big trouble," Fiona said to Chap. "What are you going to say?"

"What do you mean, *I'm* in big trouble?" Chap said. "I thought we were in this together."

"Not any more," Fiona said.

1. *During one week if 500 people play the game, and 2 are winners, how much profit will the game make?*

   _____

2. *If the game makes a profit of $0 one week, how many winners were there out of 500 players?*

   _____

3. *If 500 people play each week, what is the maximum number that can win for the game to turn a profit?*

   _____

4. *During week 19, 500 people played the game and 25 of them were winners. How much profit was this?*

   _____

5. *Can you figure out why the number of winners keeps increasing? Hint: It is not the result of "cheating" on anyone's part.*

   _____

   _____

   _____

   _____

6. *How can Chap make the game "work" again? Hint: Look back at the way the game was originally set up.*

   _____

   _____

   _____

7. *If nothing changes, predict how many winners there will be per week two months from now.*

   _____

DOREEN AND TIM ARE GOING STEADY!

Tim asked Doreen to go steady. Doreen said she would under one condition: that Tim not tell anyone for at least a week.

"I won't tell anyone if you won't," Tim said.

Doreen frowned. She *had* to tell Babs, her best friend. And Tom, her other best friend, ought to know too. "What if I promise only to tell two people?" she asked Tim.

"Fine with me," Tim said. He'd tell only two people himself—his best friends Anita and Luis.

"What if Anita and Luis each tell two people?" Doreen asked.

"I don't know," Tim said. "What if Babs and Tom do the same thing?

Maybe we better sit and think about this."

1. *If after an hour Tim and Doreen each tell their best friends, how many people will know they are going steady?*

_____

2. *If it takes an hour for each friend to tell two other friends the news, how long will it take before 30 people know about Doreen and Tim? (Assume that each person who learns the secret tells it to two different friends and only two friends, and that it takes exactly an hour for the secrets to be told.)*

_____

3. *At this rate, how long will it take the whole school—510 students— to learn what happened?*

_____

"This will never work," Tim said.

"You're right," Doreen said. "It won't work. But I've got an idea. The way it was before, we each told two friends for a total of four. Why don't we cut it down to three friends? We'll make a list—together—of three people we want to tell."

"Great," Tim said. "And each of them can only tell three other friends."

4. *Using this new arrangement, will it take more or less time before 40 people know the secret? (Assume that each person who learns the secret tells it to three different friends and only three friends, and that it takes exactly an hour for the secrets to be told.)*

_____

5. *How many hours will it take the whole school to know the secret?*

_____

6. *Suppose Tim and Doreen each told four friends the secret, but each friend could only tell one other friend. Would the secret travel more quickly or less quickly than before?*

_____

7. *How long would it take before 50 people know the secret?*

_____

EPILOGUE

Tim and Doreen never could agree on which and how many people to tell. They argued about it until Spanish class started. Someone overheard the argument and started the rumor that they were "not getting along."

In almost no time, "not getting along" changed to "breaking up."

When Doreen heard this she was furious. She waited for Tim outside Gym.

"How dare you tell everyone we broke up when we never even started going together in the first place," she said.

"How dare you blame me when I had nothing to do with it," Tim said.

Doreen looked at him closely. "Are you telling the truth?"

"Of course I am," Tim said.

"I can't believe it," said Doreen. "Someone must have started a rumor about us."

The two of them started to laugh.

When they had finished laughing, Tim became serious. He asked Doreen to go steady with him for the second time. Doreen said she would, but only if they didn't tell anyone at all. At least for a while.

"Fine with me," Tim said.

And that was how it ended—happily. Except for the fact that someone spotted them laughing and smiling together. By the next morning a new rumor had already started.

But that's another story.

WORK BACKWARDS

Toby wants to add three new laughs to her repertoire—the SNICKER, SNORT, and CACKLE. The Laugh-Meter rates a CACKLE as 5 times as funny as a SNORT. It rates a SNORT is 3 times as funny as a SNICKER. And it rates a SNICKER is 5 points less funny than a CHUCKLE. If a CHUCKLE registers 10 points on the Laugh-Meter, how funny is a CACKLE?

The best strategy here is to have students begin with what they know. What do they know? First, they know that a CHUCKLE is worth 10. Now, have them work backwards from there, until they find out what a CACKLE is worth.

Since a SNICKER is 5 points less funny than a CHUCKLE, students can connect what they know to what they don't know.

SNICKER = CHUCKLE − 5
SNICKER = 10 − 5, so ➡ SNICKER = 5

Now have them connect the SNICKER to the SNORT. They know that a SNORT is three times as funny as a SNICKER.

SNORT = 3 x SNICKER
SNORT = 3 x 5, so ➡ SNORT = 15

Finally, they know that a CACKLE is 5 times as funny as a SNORT.

CACKLE = 5 x SNORT
CACKLE = 5 x 15, so ➡ CACKLE = 75

By working backwards from what they do know, students can find out things that they don't know.

TIPS TO SHARE WITH STUDENTS

- Begin Working Backwards by making a list of what you know, what you don't know, and what you want to find out.

- Working Backwards is best for problems that contain a step-by-step process or a complicated chain of information.

- Work step by step. Keep track of what you find out.

- Evaluate what you find out. After each step, ask yourself: *Am I getting any closer to my goal?*

- Always keep an eye out for shortcuts. Work Backwards when you know the answer and are trying to figure out the question.

COMBINATIONS: Work Backwards works well with most of the other problem-solving strategies, and especially well with:

- Make a Table
- Use Easier Numbers
- Draw a Diagram

CAUTION: In some problems, steps are missing. If students try to work backwards without all the information they need, they won't be able to solve the problem.

TOBY AND THE LAUGH MACHINE

Toby had always wanted to be the best at something. But she wasn't terribly good at sports (too dull) or music (too picky-picky), and while she liked to dance, she would probably never be the "best" at it (too lanky).

The one thing she was good at was laughing. Her mother said it was a natural gift. It got to the point that folks would end up laughing *because* of Toby instead of whoever or whatever was supposed to be funny. She was that good.

From there it was only a short step to Hollywood. It seems that the Big Time Television Network needed a professional "laugher" for its audience. Toby tried out and won the job outright from 60 other contestants. From there it was on to all those hilarious Big TV shows, such as "Barney Pigg" and "I Married a

Horse," where Toby was expected to laugh up a storm.

Which she did, and quite well, thank you, until the network bosses came up with a Laughter Machine. The buttons on the machine are shown below.

Toby knew that she could beat the machine at its own game if she could

GIGGLE	3 times as funny as a CHUCKLE, scores 30 on a Laugh-Meter
GUFFAW	3 times as funny as a CHORTLE
CHORTLE	Twice as funny as a CHUCKLE
HOWL	20 points more than a GUFFAW on a Laugh-Meter
ROAR	10 times as funny as a CHUCKLE, 20 more than a HOWL on a Laugh-Meter
CHUCKLE	See GIGGLE, CHORTLE, ROAR

only get a hold of a Laugh-Meter. With a Laugh-Meter, she could measure the precise power of each laugh. But then she realized that she could figure out the value of each laugh even without a meter.

1. **Which has the greater laugh value, a GIGGLE or a CHUCKLE?**

   _____

2. **Which laugh has the largest value?**

   _____

3. **Which laugh has the smallest value?**

   _____

4. **List the laughs in the order of how funny they are.**

   _____

5. **What is the value of a CHUCKLE?**

   _____

6. **A HOWL is how many times as funny as a CHUCKLE?**

   _____

7. **What laughs combined equal the power of a ROAR?**

   _____

8. **Give the value of each laugh.**

   _____

It came down to this. Toby would have a "Laugh-Off" against the Laugh Machine. Whoever laughed more accurately would get the job as Chief Laughter for Big TV's new fall shows.

The two battled it out for hours and hours. Whenever Toby laughed, the delighted audience roared along with her, while during the machine's laugh there was an eerie silence in the room. But the machine's laughing _was_ more accurate. In the end, the machine was ahead, not by a lot, mind you, but just by a few snickers, which were almost too small to detect on a Laugh-Meter.

As the Big Boss came out to announce the winner, Toby hung her head. She had laughed her best, but she just couldn't quite compete with a machine.

"And the winner is—TOBY FRANKLIN!" the Big Boss announced. Toby was stunned.

"Why me?" she asked.

"Simple," said the Big Boss. "When the Machine laughs, it laughs by itself. But when you laugh, everyone laughs with you."

THE INCREDIBLE DO-NOTHING MACHINE

The best thing Eli Edison never invented was his own name, which was a combination of two famous inventors—Eli Whitney and Thomas Edison.

That's what Eli wanted to be—an inventor. The only trouble was, all the good inventions were already taken. Take the light bulb, for example. Or the cotton gin, Eli Whitney's invention. Both were already invented.

As for the more exotic things, like the microwave oven, the shoe horn, the thing that takes pits out of cherries, or the remote control garage door opener, Eli could only give a sigh of envy.

"If only I'd thought of that," he often said to himself.

But he hadn't. In fact, the only things he ever seemed to think of were either already thought of, like the spark-plug wrench, or not worth thinking of, like magnetic breakfast cereal, or electric trousers.

Then one day he was sitting in his invention laboratory with his dog Rolf when he hit upon an idea.

"Eureka!" he cried, which is inventor talk for "It's about time!"

And he showed the invention to Rolf, who wasn't impressed, but then the only things that ever seemed to impress Rolf were leftovers, hot dogs, and other dogs.

"Well aren't you even going to ask me what it's called?" Eli asked the dog. "Okay, I'll tell you. It's called the The Incredible Do-Nothing Machine. You want to see how it works?"

Rolf barked, which Eli took as encouragement, so he showed him this diagram.

INSTRUCTIONS

A. First think of Your Number. Then stick it in the machine.

B. Multiply Your Number by 3. Call this Number B.

C. Subtract Your Number from Number B, to get Number C.

D. Divide Number C by .05 to get Number D.

E. Add Number D to 10 times Your

Number. Now you have Number E.

F. Figure out what 1 percent of Number E equals. Call this Number F.

G. Add Number F to the age you turned (or will turn) on your birthday this year. Then add the last two digits of the year you were

born. Now you have Number G.

H. Subtract the last two digits of the current year from Number G to get Number H.

I. Multiply Number H times 2 and there you have it! Your have Your Number!

	ELI'S MACHINE	USING THE NUMBER 12
A.	Your Number	12
B.	Your Number x 3 = Number B	12 x 3 =36
C.	Number B − Your Number = Number C	36 − 12 = 24
D.	Number C ÷ .05 = Number D	24 ÷ .05 = 480
E.	Number D + 10 x Your Number = Number E	480 + 10 x 12 (=120) = 600
F.	1% of Number E = Number F	1% of 600 = 6
G.	Number F + your age (on this year's birthday) + year you were born =Number G	6 + Eli's age (10) + year Eli was born (82) =98
H.	Number G - last two digits of current year = Number H	98 − 92 (current year) = 6
I.	Number H x 2 = Your Number	6 x 2 12

1. *Test out Eli's Machine with your own number. Does it work? Why do you think he calls it a "Do-Nothing" machine?*

_____

_____

_____

_____

2. *After a while Eli's machine began to malfunction. He plugged in the number 8 and came out with an answer of 800. Which step in the process did the machine leave out?*

_____

3. *Another malfunction had the machine starting with the number 40 and jamming, leaving a value of 1600. After what step did the machine jam?*

_____

Eli was feeling pretty good about the Machine until he brought it to the 33rd Annual Invention Convention. There he saw hundreds of inventions.

He saw cups of coffee that poured themselves. Cows that milked themselves. Televisions that changed their own channels. Books that turned their own pages. Even a pair of tiny windshield de-foggers for people who wore glasses.

The one thing that all the machines had in common was that they Did Something. Eli's invention was the only thing there that did Absolutely Nothing.

And that meant it would never win the Best Invention prize. What good was a Do-Nothing machine compared to something useful like a talking pencil or an electric ear massager?

"Are you kidding?" a man said to him. "You don't know how tired I am of inventions that DO THINGS. Automatic this, electric that—who CARES? You know what I mean?"

When Eli confessed that he did not know, the man introduced himself.

"My name's Barney Hart," he said. "I'm rich and I'm spoiled and I've been searching my entire life for something to do when I don't particularly feel like doing anything."

"What do you normally do when you don't particularly feel like doing anything?" Eli asked.

"I play a lot of solitaire," Barney Hart said. "I drum my fingers on the table."

"Sounds dull," Eli said.

"It *is* dull," Barney said. "Show me how this works."

So Eli showed him.

"Great," Barney said. "I'll take 10,000 of them."

"Excuse me," Eli said. "Did you say 10,000?"

He had said 10,000. For Barney Hart may have been rich and spoiled, but he was by no means a stupid man. He bought 10,000 of the Incredible Do-Nothing Machines and sold them in his Barney's Barn Drug Stores.

He even made up a slogan for them: "The Incredible Do-Nothing Machine: The perfect thing to do when you don't particularly feel like doing anything."

As for Eli, he got sort of rich himself, and used the money to invent other Do-Nothing Machines, including the Electric Do-Nothing Machine, which did nothing electrically, the Automatic Do-Nothing Machine, which did nothing all by itself so you didn't have to bother with it, and finally, for Rolf, the Automatic Digital Do-Nothing Machine for Dogs, which automatically and digitally did nothing for a dog without even waking him up.

YOUR TURN

Invent your own Incredible, Astounding Do-Nothing Machine. Then "break" the machine by changing one of the steps. Trade machines with a classmate. See if you can discover the mistake in each other's machine.

TRIVIAL COURT

BAILIFF: Your Honor, we call Defendant Timmy Moran, accused of Trivial Crime Number 403: LEAVING THE BATHROOM LIGHT ON ALL NIGHT.

JUDGE: How does the defendant plead?

TIMMY: Not guilty, your honor. I didn't do it. And anyway, so what if I *did* leave the bathroom light on? What's the harm? I'm just a kid.

JUDGE: The court would like to remind the defendant of the extremely trivial nature of these proceedings. Now, would the prosecution like to call its first witness?

PROSECUTOR: We would, Your Honor. Prosecution calls Mrs. Marjorie Moran, the defendant's mother. Mrs. Moran, do you swear to tell the truth, whole truth, and nothing but the truth no matter how insignificant?

MRS. MORAN: I do.

PROSECUTOR: Mrs. Moran, can you describe what you saw and did on the morning of March 3?

MRS. MORAN: Well, I got up early that day, put on my fuzzy-wuzzy slippers, and....

DEFENSE: Objection! Your Honor. What relevance do a pair of fuzzy-wuzzy slippers have in this case?

JUDGE: Objection sustained. Get to the point, Prosecutor Phelps.

PROSECUTOR: When you got to the bathroom, Mrs. Moran, what did you see?

MRS. MORAN: The light was on.

PROSECUTOR: I have nothing further for this witness, Your Honor.

JUDGE: Defense?

DEFENSE: Mrs. Moran, let's go back to the previous evening of March 2. Did you SEE Timmy leave the light on?

MRS. MORAN: Well, no, but I did hear him click the lights. He was playing with the switch, and I told him to stop. My husband was making a videotape of our dog playing the xylophone.

JUDGE: Your dog plays the xylophone?

MRS. MORAN: Yes, Your Honor. Her name is Fifi. We want her to go on the TV program, "The World's Most Hilarious Stupid Pet Tricks."

JUDGE: Oh, yes. I love that show. It just cracks me up. Did you see the tap-dancing parrot?

MRS. MORAN: Why yes I did. Wasn't that wonderful, Your Honor?

DEFENSE: Sorry to interrupt, Your Honor, but can we get on with it here? At this point I'd like to introduce Mr. Moran's videotape. As you can tell, the bathroom is not visible in this scene. But you can clearly hear Timmy clicking the light switch 43 times. Now Mrs. Moran, can you recall whether the light switch was on or off when Timmy entered the bathroom?

PROSECUTOR: Objection, Your Honor! Relevance. What does it matter whether the light was on or off when Timmy started clicking?

DEFENSE Your Honor, if the State fails to establish whether that light was on or off to begin with, then there is no way they can prove that my client left it on.

JUDGE: Are you suggesting that there was ANOTHER suspect who might have turned on the bathroom light, Mr. Fox?

DEFENSE: It's possible, Your Honor.

PROSECUTOR: I strongly object to this whole line of questioning, Your Honor.

JUDGE: Thirty minute recess! (SLAMMING GAVEL) Both counselors see me in my chambers.

1. *If the bathroom light was ON to begin with, would it be ON or off after Timmy clicked it 2 times?*

   _____

2. *Again assuming the light was ON to start, would it be ON or OFF after:*

   4 clicks? _____

   6 clicks? _____

   12 clicks? _____

   40 clicks? _____

3. *How would your answers change if the light in Problems 1 and 2 started out OFF?*

   _____

   _____

4. *If the light switch was in the ON position before Timmy got to the bathroom, did he leave it on when he left?*

_____

5. *Suppose Timmy had clicked the light 356 times instead of 43 times. Would your answer change? Why?*

_____

_____

6. *Suppose the bathroom had a three-way switch with positions as shown on right. If the switch started from the OFF position, what position would it be in after 42 clicks?*

(Assume that first click is to right and no position is skipped.)

_____

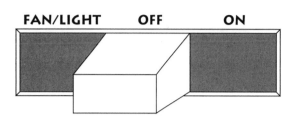

7. *In what position would the switchs in problem 6 be after:*

(A) *23 clicks?* _____

(B) *33 clicks?* _____

(C) *43 clicks?* _____

(D) *77 clicks?* _____

NAME _____

BURGER BATTLES

Just about everything about Russell's Burger Universe was better than Plain Jane's Burger Basement. The burgers were better, the service was better, the decorations were better, even the parking lot was better. So why did Plain Jane sell so many more hamburgers?

"Beats me," Russell said. Then one day he thought he'd found the answer: Jane's secret sauce.

"I've just got to find out the recipe to her secret sauce," Russell said. So he got a hold of a Plain Jane hamburger and analyzed the ingredients.

1. *In one sample Russell found that there was 3/8 ounces of mustard to every 1 1/2 ounces of mayonnaise. What is the simplest whole number ratio between the two ingredients?*

————————————————

————————————————

2. *In that same sample he found that there was 3 times as much ketchup as mustard. Does the sauce have more mayonnaise or ketchup?*

————————————————

————————————————

3. *What is the simplest whole number ratio between mayonnaise and ketchup?*

————————————————

————————————————

4. *The ratio of honey to mustard was the same as the ratio of ketchup to mayonnaise. What is the whole number ratio between mayonnaise and honey?*

————————————————

————————————————

5. *Write the recipe for the secret sauce without using any fractions.*

————————————————

6. *Russell wants to make 70 ounces of secret sauce. How many ounces of honey does he need?*

————————————————

7. *Russell has 50 ounces of mayonnaise, 36 ounces of ketchup, 12 ounces of mustard, and 10*

ounces of honey. How much secret sauce can he make?

_____

8. *How many ounces of each ingredient will be left over in Problem 7?*

_____

_____

_____

EPILOGUE

After Russell figured out the recipe for Jane's secret sauce, he began slathering it on his burgers and, sure enough, his business grew by leaps and bounds. In fact, he soon began to attract most of Plain Jane's clientele.

When Jane heard of Russell's new-found popularity, she decided the time was ripe to conduct a competitive analysis of her own to find out what accounted for Russell's success. After much snooping and nibbling, she determined that the only thing the two establishments had in common was the secret sauce. Customers were flocking to Russell's Burger Universe for one simple reason: it was better. In order to increase business, all she had to do was copy everything about his place.

And so she did. She upgraded her burgers, service, decor, and even added twelve new spots to the parking lot. She also changed her place's name from Plain Jane Burgers to Jane's Burger Universe. And as you may have guessed, in no time flat, she had twice as many customers.

When Russell caught wind of Jane's improvements and increased popularity, he knew he was in no position to gripe. After all, he'd copied Jane's secret sauce *first*. So the two Burger Universes peacefully coexisted—each attracting the exact same number of customers. All's fair in burgers and business.

THE FISH PEOPLE

Our number system is based on our fingers. Prehistoric mathematicians noticed that we had TEN of them, so they created corresponding numbers: 1 2 3 4 5 6 7 8 9 10.

Recently, scientists discovered a civilization of Fish People. They based their numbering system not on fingers, but on fishing.

The Fish People cared about only one thing—fishing. They fished in boats *that could fit exactly five people.* Any more was too many. Any fewer was not enough.

NUMBER		FISH PEOPLE'S NUMBER
1	=	NOT MANY
2	=	NOT ENOUGH
3	=	STILL NOT ENOUGH
4	=	REALLY CLOSE TO ENOUGH
5	=	ENOUGH
6	=	TOO MANY
7	=	WAY TOO MANY
8	=	WAY, WAY TOO MANY
9	=	THIS BOAT'S ABOUT TO SINK
10	=	LET'S GET ANOTHER BOAT

The names of the numbers in their system are on the chart below.

The following problems are based on the "Fish Number" system. When you do the problems, just remember that Fish People have only two goals:

(A) to get ENOUGH people to fill a boat;

(B) once that boat is filled, to be able to say "LET'S GET ANOTHER BOAT."

Mr. Trout got in the boat. "Who wants to go fishing?" he asked.

"How many are going so far?" Mrs. Guppy asked.

"NOT MANY. Just me," Mr. Trout said.

1. *How many people are in the boat?*

———————————————

2. *Soon afterward, Mrs. Guppy's family arrived. She has NOT MANY husbands, and NOT ENOUGH children. Including Mrs. Guppy, how many are in the Guppy family?*

———————————————

3. *If Mrs. Guppy's family joins Mr. Trout in the boat, how many people will there be in "Fish Numbers?"*

———————————————

The Tuna Family came by. There were REALLY CLOSE TO ENOUGH of them, but when they got in the boat, Mr. Trout said, "There are WAY, WAY TOO MANY of us here."

Mrs. Tuna stood up. "That's not right!" she cried. "In fact, THIS BOAT'S ABOUT TO SINK!"

4. *Who is right?*

———————————————

5. *How may people does the Tuna family need to have its own boat?*

———————————————

6. *The Perch family came by. "Oh no," Mrs. Tuna said, "TOO MANY of you will not be able to go with our family on a boat." However, since NOT MANY of you can join us, then there should be ENOUGH of you to fill your own boat, with NOT MANY left over. In "Fish Numbers," how many people are in the Perch family?*

———————————————

7. *If a group of WAY, WAY TOO MANY Fish People meets a group with REALLY CLOSE TO ENOUGH Fish People, how many boats can they fill, with how many Fish People left over.*

———————————————

8. *Some Fish People posed for a portrait. They stood in REALLY CLOSE TO ENOUGH rows and NOT ENOUGH columns. In "Fish Numbers," how many people were there in all?*

———————————————

YOUR TURN

Make up your own problem using the "Fish Numbers."

LIFESTYLES OF THE RICH AND SUPERSTITIOUS

Rumor had it that Oswald Doggett was one of the world's most superstitious men. But was he also dangerous? That's what my editor sent me to find out.

My name is Maud Martinez. I'm a reporter for the *Daily Sun*. I'd heard the weird stories about Doggett and his 100-story Doggett Building. How the elevators were "haunted." How people could get lost in there for weeks at a time. How Doggett's strange superstitions were the cause of the whole thing. But as a professional reporter I made it my business to hold off judgment until I knew the facts. That's what I went to the Doggett Building for—to get the facts.

Right off I noticed something strange about the elevator. Instead of just pushing the button of your floor, you pushed the number of how many floors *up or down* you wanted to go. For example, to go 5 floors up you pushed +5. To go 4 floors down you pushed –4.

So far, so good. I was on floor 1, so I pushed +6 to go to floor 7. A strange man greeted me at the door.

"Can I help you?" he said, with a sneering smile. He was wearing a janitor's uniform.

"I'm Maud Martinez," I said. "Reporter for the *Sun*. I was looking

for the 7th floor. I think I'm lost."

"Oh, think nothing of it, Ms. Martinez," the man said, still smiling. "Everyone gets lost looking for the 7th floor because there *is* no 7th floor."

"Why not?" I asked.

"Mr. Doggett believes 7 is an unlucky number," he said. "Also 13. Or any number that divides evenly by 7 or 13. Also, the 'twin' numbers like 22, 33, and so on. None of those floors exist on this elevator."

"You're joking," I said.

"Mr. Doggett never jokes," the man said. His face seemed frozen in that sinister smile. I decided I'd better leave. I hopped back in the elevator and pushed +20.

Now I was lost.

1. *On what "floor" did Maud meet the strange man?*

_____

2. *What was the actual floor?*

_____

3. *What "floor" did Maud end up on?*

_____

4. *What was the actual floor?*

_____

When the door opened, I walked out and there was the same man again. How had he gotten there so fast? What did he want? I'll admit it: I, Maud Martinez, didn't feel like sticking around to find out. I was spooked. I panicked and pushed the button. I don't even know what button I pushed, but when the elevator stopped I got out and found myself on the 96th floor. Now I had to get down.

I figured that since I was on the 96th floor I should push –95 to get to the lobby on floor 1. When I did, the elevator readout said TRY AGAIN and refused to move.

5. *Why did the elevator refuse to move?*

_____

_____

6. *Should Maud have pushed a smaller or a larger number to get down to the lobby?*

_____

7. *What number should Maud push to get down to the first floor?*

_____

8. *How many floors does the Doggett Building have?*

_____

When I finally got down, I ran straight to my office and searched through the files for a picture of Doggett. When I finally located one I almost dropped. That strange man I kept running into—that was Doggett! I should have known it would be something like that.

Now I had to write my story. Was Doggett just a harmless, superstitious prankster? Or was there something more behind that phony grin plastered on his face. Was it all in my mind, or was there something really sinister going on over there?

I peered out my window at the "100-story" Doggett Building in the distance. Somehow it seemed to be mocking me. Or was it my imagination?

ANNOTATED SOLUTIONS

SPORTS BLAB WITH BUZZ BUSBY (PAGE 15)

1. 4 of 12 or 1/3.

2. .333.

3. Terry "Big Tuna" Templeton is batting .250. His average is .083 lower than "Homerun" Hornsby's.

4. 4. See the Guess and Check strategy on page 13 for hints on how to solve this problem.

5. 9.

6. 4.

7. .414.

8. Slightly under .500. "Homerun" Hornsy is two hits short of .500 now. So he will still be two hits short at the end of the season, no matter how many times he bats.

MORRIE'S MORE OF EVERYTHING SHOP (PAGE 17)

1. 3 1/2 minutes; 3 1/2 minutes.

2. Many answers including: 3 green, 1 yellow.

3. 1 green, 3 yellow, 6 white. Guess and Check is the strategy of choice for this problem. Since Morrie saved a total of 3 1/2 minutes, you can rule out using any red or blue beads. Why? To find the beads Morrie did use, just Guess then Check. For example:

> **GUESS 1:** Suppose he used 3 green beads. This means the remaining 7 beads must total 30 seconds. Is this possible? No. So try again.
>
> **GUESS 2:** Suppose he used 1 green bead and 4 yellows. That makes a total of 1 minute (1 green) plus 2 minutes (four yellow). The remaining 5 beads must total 30 seconds again. This won't work. Adjust your guess again.
>
> **GUESS 3:** 1 green (1 minute) + 3 yellows (1 1/2 minutes = 2 1/2 minutes. The remaining 6 beads must total 1 minute. Will this work? Yes, if you choose 6 white beads, totalling 60 seconds. So your answer is: 1 green, 3 yellow, 6 white.

4. 4 times.

5. 5 1/4 minutes. Use Easier Numbers is a good strategy here. Suppose Morrie started with 8 minutes instead of 7. In Problem 1 he worked twice as fast, saving 4 of the 8 minutes, leaving him 4 minutes. Now, he works twice as fast again,

saving 2 minutes. He is left with 2 minutes from the original 8, meaning that he's saved 6 minutes total.

Now, use the same procedure starting with 7 minutes instead of 8. 7 is reduced to 3 1/2. 3 1/2 is reduced to 1 3/4. Subtract 1 3/4 from 7 gives a total saving of 5 1/4 minutes.

6. Prudence Sneff wants twice as much time as on the first day, or the whole 7 minutes. The only way to save 7 minutes would be to sweep in no time at all. This is impossible. To save 7 minutes, Morrie needs to take a longer task (e.g., washing the windows) and do it faster than normal.

7. More than one answer including: 2 green, 1 yellow, 1 white.

8. More than one answer including: 3 of each color. Guess and Check. Start with 1 of each color, 3 and so on.

WHAT PLANET AM I FROM? (PAGE 19)

NOTE: Students must know that there are 8 ounces in a half-pound.

1. No. Gravity on Joe-09's planet must be less than Earth's, not more.

2. Mercury. Multiply 8 (oz.) by .28 and you get 2.24.

3. 14 lbs.

4. Both the same.

5. The kilogram bucket, because kg's weigh more than pounds.

6. 60 lbs.

7. 2.63. From the chart, Earth gravity is 1.0; Mars is 0.38. This means that Earth's force is 2.63 times that of Mars. If Mars were given a value of 1.0, it should be obvious that Earth would have a value of 2.63.

8. Uranus. If Mars has a value of 1.0, what planet would have gravity that is 2.89 times as powerful? Look at the chart. See if there is a planet that has 2.89 times as much gravity as Mars. Uranus is the answer because 0.38 X 2.89 = 1.0982 or about1.1, the value of Uranus.

FROG GETS A TELEPHONE (PAGE 21)

1. More than one answer including: even numbers counting backwards from 10.

2. 0; 108-6420.

3. No. Numbers may form patterns, but there is no guarantee that a phone number will follow one.

4. 10 possible numbers: 108-6420, 108-6421, 108-6422, 108-6423, 108-6424, 108-6425, 108-6426, 108-6427, 108-6428, 108-6429.

5. 8.

6. Start with 14, take half, that's the next number, then go down by two, take half again, and so on.

7. 147-126-1058.

8. 4, 6, 3, 4.

9. Beginning with 3, each number in counting order is followed by the square of that number; the complete sequence should be: 39416525636749.

SOAPS (PAGE 23)

NOTE: Students must know that the probability of two independent events occurring is the product of their individual probabilities.

1. **A:** 1/4

   B: 1/8. The probability of Quentin Crowe being evil is 1/2, and of him being a doctor is 1/4. Therefore the probability of him being an evil doctor is 1/4 X 1/2 = 1/8

   C: 1/2,304.

2. **A:** 3/4.
   B: 1/16.
   C: 1/108.

3. **A:** 48.

   B: 40.

   C: 1.

4. **A:** Yes.

   B: Yes.

   C: No.

   D: No.

5. 9.

6. Harley could be good looking, jealous and: evil, rich, no good, or well dressed; good looking, a fool and: evil, rich, no good, or well dressed; or he could be a good-looking hairdresser.

7. 5/48.

8. 1/16.

THE FARMER AND THE VISITOR (PAGE 25)

1. 28 carpet squares.

2. 6 feet by 6 feet.

3. More than one answer including: 12 feet by 12 feet and 6 feet by 6 feet.

4. More than one answer including: six 12 feet by 12 feet squares and four 6 feet by 6 feet squares.

5. Three sheets. The diagram below shows one way to position the three sheets.

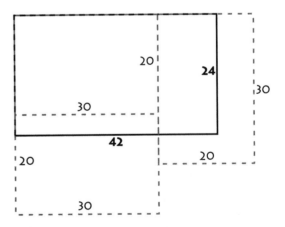

6. Many answers including: 7 feet by 4 feet.

7. More than one answer including: 14 feet by 12 feet.

THE FABULOUS RAPPOZIS (PAGE 29)

1. 40 lbs.

2. 130 lbs.

3. 230 lbs.

4. 330 lbs.

5. 480 lbs.

6. 25:48.

7. Victor can lift almost two times his body weight.

8. Magda. Pound for pound means: if Victor and Magda weighed the same, who would be able to lift more? To see how Use Easier Numbers works for this problem see the Use Easier Number strategy on page 27.

9. No, she'd have to leave out Baby.

SYLVESTER JAMES LEE (PAGE 32)

NOTE: Ratios and proportions are useful for solving the problems in this story.

1. 305 units.

2. 3,660.

3. 6 years old.

4. About 25 units.

5. More than one answer, including: 9,150, his 30th birthday.

6. He's gone to the time before he was born.

7. About four months before he was born. When a VCR rewinds, it hits 0000, then 9,999, then 9,998, etc. So 9,900 is 99 units, or about 4 months before Sylvester was born.

NOSE JOB (PAGE 34)

NOTE: Ratios and proportions are especially helpful for this story.

1. Find the ratio in height of Bill to his shadow. The ratio of the statue to its shadow should be the same.

2. 2 2/5.

3. 2 2/5.

4. 36 feet. Use Easier Numbers lets you see what is happening in this problem. Suppose Bill's shadow was 3 feet instead of 2 1/2 feet. That would mean the he would be twice as tall as his shadow. That would also mean that the statue would be twice as tall as its shadow. The actual numbers show that the ratio between Bill and his shadow is 2.4 to 1. The ratio for the statue should be the same. Multiplying 15 (the length of the statue's shadow) by 2.4 gives you an answer of 36 feet.

5. 1 foot.

6. About 2 cubes.

7. 432 cubes. Drawing a Diagram helps you see the relationship between heights and nose sizes. Bill is 6 feet tall; the statue is 36 feet tall (Problem 4). This means in every dimension—height, width, and length, the statue should be 6 times

the size of Bill. Bill's nose is 2 inches by 1 inch by 1 inch. The statue's nose, therefore, should be 12 by 6 by 6 inches. In volume this comes out to 12 X 6 X 6 = 432 square inches.

8. 108 lbs.

THE EXAGGERATED NEWS (PAGE 36)

NOTE: Kids need to know that presidential elections occur every four years and the Declaration of Independence was written in 1776. They should also be familiar with the film *20,000 Leagues Under the Sea.*

1. Channels on which EXAGGERATED NEWS is seen: 5.

2. Pinky's actual weight: 22 lbs.

3. Hours Pinky spent in the tree: 168.

4. Last time Pinky was seen: 4 years earlier.

5. Number of mice: 39.

6. Pinky's IQ: 86.

7. Number of pounds of catnip Pinky has: 346.

8. Cat population: 65,000.

9. Number of City Council members: 20.

10. Votes received: 11.

11. Actual provision: 1222.

12. Declaration of Independence year: 1776.

13. Time spent sniffing: 60 percent.

14. Dog life-span: 12 years.

15. Time of Midnight Movie: 12 o'clock.

16. Movie title: *20,000 Leagues Under the Sea.*

THE CIRCLES (PAGE 39)

NOTE: Kids must know formulas for area and circumference of a circle for this story. Assume $\pi = 3.14$ and round decimals to nearest hundredth while calculating. Answers below are further rounded to nearest tenth.

1. About 6.3 inches.

2. About 4.0 inches.

3. About 28.1 inches. When his radius increased by an inch, he went from an area of about 49.7 square inches to 77.9 square inches.

4. They will both increase in circumference by about 3.14 inches.

5. Bob's will increase more. Bob will gain about 13.3 inches in area, Danny about 7.0 square inches.

6. About 8.4 inches.

7. About 18.8 inches.

8. 16 inches by 10 inches. Use Draw a Diagram to show how large a rectangle the Circles need. Grid paper helps students to be accurate here (see diagram on page 98).

9. About 41 square inches. To compute wasted space, find the sum of the Circle's area: 78.5 + 28.3 + 12.6 = about 119 square inches, and the area of rectangle: 16 X 10 = 160 square inches. Then subtract

the area of the Circles from the area of the rectangle: 160 – 119 = 41 square inches.

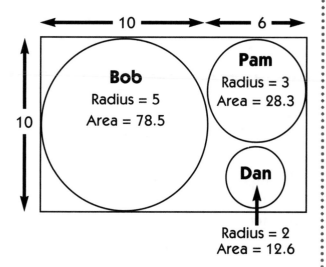

10. The Circle-500.

LUCY TRIANGLES (PAGE 43)

1. The triangle, as proposed, is impossible. The two shorter legs together do not exceed the length of the third leg.

2. Stripes or goats.

3. Many answers including: increase goats by 10, decrease stars by 10. The key to this problem (and others in this story) is to realize that the sum of the two short sides must be greater than the long side. There are many ways to accomplish this. For example, stars could be decreased by 10, and goats could be increased by 10.

   100 stars ➡ 90 stars
   66 stripes ➡ 66 stripes
   33 goats ➡ 43 goats

4. Stripes and goats. If you add and subtract the same amounts from stripes and goats, the sum of their lengths will still be shorter than 100. For example, if you add 10 goats, and subtract 10 from stripes:

   100 stars ➡ 100 stars
   66 stripes ➡ 56 stripes
   33 goats ➡ 43 goats

   66 + 43 = 99, which is less than 100 – the number of stars.

5. It won't be a triangle; the figure will not be closed.

6. The goat or stripe side.

7. Doubling the stripe side would create a very skinny triangle.

8. The goat side.

SHA LING AND THE THREE WISHES (PAGE 45)

1. 2.

2. 5.

3. 0.

4. 9.

5. 27.

6. Many possible answer including: No, because as of now, Sha can get an infinite number of wishes.

7. 4.

THE LEAKY TOP CORPORATION (PAGE 47)

1. Triangle.

2. Square.

3. Triangle.

4. Pentagon. Diagrams and/or models can help you recognize that the greater the number of sides on the top, the smaller the total gap area. Compare, for example, an equilateral triangle to a hexagon. The hexagon is much closer to a circular shape. If you are not convinced by this example, compare the equilateral triangle to a 10-sided regular polygon. Notice, the more sides there are, the closer the shape comes to approximating a circle.

5. 8-sided figure.

6. The maximum gap would be about 0.9 inches, so they wouldn't leak out. Without algebra, the only reliable way to measure these gaps is to make a good scale model. The model shows the gaps to be about 0.9 inches in maximum width.

7. Yes, because the maximum gap is over 1/2 inch.

8. Any answer close to 3.6 inches in diameter. Without using a model, a good way to find this is to subtract the area of the square (4.25 X 4.25 =18) from the area of the circle (3.14 X 5 squared = 28.3), to give an area of all four gaps of about 10 square includes (28–18=10).Use the area formula again to find the radius of a circle with an area of 10. This gives a circle with a radius of about 1.8. This circle would have a diameter of twice the radius, or about 3.6, meaning any marble with a smaller diameter would fit.

GHENGIS IN LOVE (PAGE 49)

NOTE: Graph paper is helpful, but not essential for solving these problems.

1. No.

2. 4 large units.

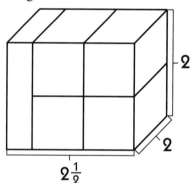

3. 40 small units.

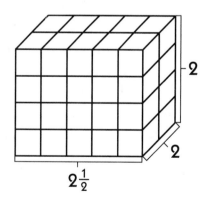

4. 12 total units; 4 large, 8 small.

5. More than one answer including: 4

large units arranged vertically, 8
small units laid horizontally over
them.

6. There are many ways to design a
box to hold all the units. The 3 foot
by 2 1/2 foot by 2 foot box is shown
below. It would have an empty
space of 1/2 a foot by 2 1/2 feet by 2
feet. This comes to a volume of: 1/2
x 2 1/2 x 2 = 2 1/2 cubic feet.

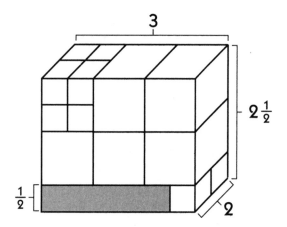

THE DOGFINDERS (PAGE 52)

• • • • • • • • • • • • • • • • • • • •

NOTE: Graph paper is helpful, but
not essential for solving these
problems.

1. 4. Draw a Diagram is essential for
this problem. The best kind of
diagram is made on a grid, like the
one shown. The four possible
locations for 4-6 are shown. Similar
diagrams can be used to solve the
other problems in the story.

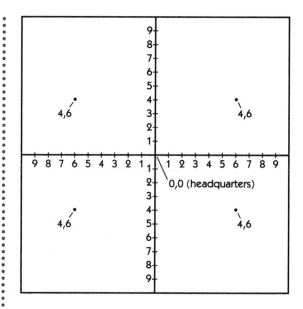

2. Farther.

3. Yes, same distance away. Measure
the distance from headquarters to
point 8-6 and point 6-8. You'll see
that they are the same.

4. He's somewhere south of the main
office. Carol has moved 3 blocks
south and the location changed
from 6-8 to 3-8. In other words, the
north-south number dropped from
6 to 3. This means that moving
south gets her closer to Snarfy.
Therefore, Snarfy must be south of
headquarters. If he had been north
of headquarters, moving south
would have increased his north-
south number to 9. (Test this for
yourself). The same basic idea
applies for problems 6 and 7.

5. 2 possible locations.

6. He's 6 blocks south and 8 blocks
west of the main office.

7. 6-5.

ROMANCE FOOTBALL (PAGE 54)

1. 7 seconds.

2. 5 yards.

3. Rob will be Daphne's 40-yard line; Rob will be on Daphne's 25-yard line.

4. At Daphne's 35-yard line, 35 yards from where Rob is now.

5. 3.5 seconds.

6. About 54 yards. Using a diagram, like the one below, it is not difficult to do this problem without algebra.

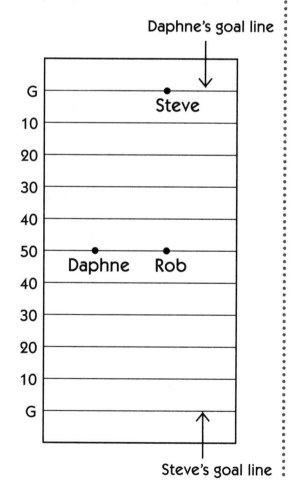

Daphne's goal line

Steve

Daphne   Rob

Steve's goal line

LOST ON NOWHERE (PAGE 56)

1. 96 miles.

2. Decrease.

3. 4 miles per hour.

4. Earth spins at about 1,000 mph; Nowhere at 4 mph, meaning Earth is about 250 times faster.

5. 20 miles. The distance around Nowhere is still the same as it was before: 80 miles. Only now, it is divided up into 4 flat faces instead of one smooth circle.

6. 8,000 cubic miles.

A THOUSAND CLOCKS (PAGE 61)

1. 24 hours. Making a table like the one shown below helps for this problem and many of the others in this story. If you continue this pattern you will see that it takes 24 hours for the clock to read the right time again.

Real Time	Gwynn's Time
12:00	12:00
1:00	1:30
2:00	3:00
3:00	4:30
4:00	6:00
5:00	7:30
6:00	9:00
7:00	10:30
8:00	12:00

2. 24 hours.

3. 72 hours.

4. The same.

5. Increase.

6. Make it gain or lose a very small amount of time every hour.

7. 4:45.

THE FOUR TOOTHBRUSHES (PAGE 64)

1. $20,000.

2. $10,000.

3. $30,000

4. Deal B. They both pay the same amount if enough CD's are sold. However, Deal B is actually better since it guarantees the Toothbrushes $20,000 even if they don't sell 20,000 CD's, which Deal A doesn't.

5. $100,000, $439,000.

6. Assuming all the CD's sell for $10 and at least 10,000 are sold under Deal A or 20,000 under Deal B, they earn exactly $1 per CD sold. Notice the pattern between the numbers in problem 5. If they sell 100,000 CD's, they earn $100,000. If they sell 439,000 CD's, they earn $439,000. Just to make sure, try a few other numbers to see if the pattern holds up. It does. The Four Toothbrushes earn exactly $1 for every CD sold.

BIRTHA BIXTON AND HER BELOVED PURPLE CALCULATOR (PAGE 66)

1. 8. It is best to Make a Table like the one below to keep track of the digits as you find them.

NUMBERS ON CALCULATOR	
Buttons	Real Numbers
0	?
1	3
2	8
3	?
4	?
5	?
6	?
7	?
8	?
9	?

2. 0.

3. 5.

4. 9.

5. 4.

6. 1.

7. 7.

8. 6.

9. 2.

THE MONDAY BLUES (PAGE 69)

1. 6.

2. Tuesday; Thursday. These two

calendars for December show how to determine on which day of the week December 9th will fall:

REAL 7-DAY WEEK

DECEMBER

S	M	T	W	T	F	S
	1	2	3	4	5	6
7	8	(9)	10	11	12	13
14	15	16	17	18	19	20
21	22	23	24	25	26	27
28	29	30	31			

BAXTER 6-DAY WEEK

DECEMBER

S	T	W	T	F	S
	1	2	3	4	5
6	7	8	(9)	10	11
12	13	14	15	16	17
18	19	20	21	22	23
24	25	26	27	28	29
30	31				

3. Wednesday.

BAXTER 6-DAY WEEK

JANUARY

S	T	W	T	F	S
		(1)	2	3	4
5	6	7	8	9	10
11	12	13	14	15	16
17	18	19	20	21	22
23	24	25	26	27	28
29	30	31			

4. None. The day of the week was different, but it still came 31 days after December 1.

REAL 7-DAY WEEK

JANUARY

S	M	T	W	T	F	S
				1	2	3
4	5	6	7	8	9	10
11	12	13	14	15	16	17
18	19	20	21	22	23	24
25	26	27	28	29	30	31

5. 2 more days in December; 1 more in January.

6. 2 fewer in December; 1 fewer in January.

7. They lost 3 weekdays in two months, or between 1 and 2 weekdays per month. At this rate, over 6 1/2 months from December to the middle of June they'll lose about 10 weekdays. This will make summer vacation about 2 weeks late in "real" calendar terms. Expect answers to vary for this problem, since they are estimates.

THE CRYSTAL BEAN-POT LOTTERY (PAGE 71)

1. $300.

2. 5.

3. 4.

4. The game lost $2,000.

5. The winners are putting their beans back into the pot. The losers are not. In other words, the number of losing beans is decreasing, and the number of winning beans is staying the same, so the chances of choosing a winning bean are increasing.

6. Make the losers put their bean back in the pot.

7. Everyone will be a winner. All of the losing beans will be discarded by then, leaving only winners.

DOREEN AND TIM ARE GOING STEADY! (PAGE 73)

1. 6, including Doreen and Tim.

2. 3 hours. A tree diagram works extremely well for this problem. The one below shows that after 3 hours, 30 people know about the secret, including Tim and Doreen.

3. 7 hours. Extend the tree diagram to get the answer to this problem. The table below shows how many people know the secret after each hour that passes. Notice that if you add all the new people together you get the total number of people for any hour. For example, after 3 hours there are: 2 + 4 + 8 + 16 = 30 total people.

Hour	New People This Hour	Total People
0	2	2
1	4	6
2	8	14
3	16	30
4	32	62
5	64	126
6	128	254
7	256	510

4. Less.

5. The number of people who know

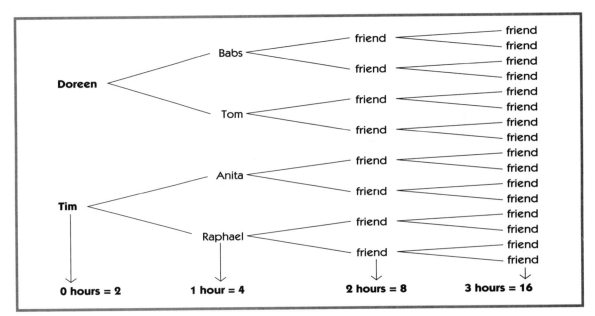

0 hours = 2   1 hour = 4   2 hours = 8   3 hours = 16

the secret doesn't exceed 510 until 6 hours pass.

Hour	New People This Hour	Total People
0	2	2
1	3	5
2	9	14
3	27	41
4	81	122
5	243	365
6	729	1094

6. Less quickly.

7. 6 hours.

TOBY AND THE LAUGH MACHINE (PAGE 77)

1. GIGGLE.

2. ROAR.

3. CHUCKLE.

4. CHUCKLE, CHORTLE, GIGGLE, GUFFAW, HOWL, ROAR.

5. 10.

6. 8.

7. 2 Answers: CHUCKLE, GIGGLE, GUFFAW or CHORTLE, HOWL.

8. ROAR – 100, HOWL – 80, GUFFAW – 60, GIGGLE – 30, CHORTLE – 20, CHUCKLE – 10.

THE INCREDIBLE DO-NOTHING MACHINE (PAGE 79)

1. Because it does nothing.

2. Step F.

3. After Step D.

TRIVIAL COURT (PAGE 83)

1. ON.

2. ON, ON, ON, ON.

3. Every answer would be the opposite—OFF.

4. Timmy did not leave it ON.

5. Yes. Any even number would change the answer.

6. OFF.

4. A: FAN/LIGHT.

B: ON.

C: FAN/LIGHT.

D: ON.

BURGER BATTLES (PAGE 86)

1. 4 mayo to 1 mustard. Use Easier Numbers. Suppose there were 2 ounces of mustard to every 6 ounces of mayo. The ratio of mayo to mustard would be 6/2, or 6 divided by 2, which equals 3. Now you know to divide ounces of mayo, 1 1/2, by the ounces of mustard, 3/8. 1 1/2 divided by 3/8 = 4.

2. Mayo.

3. 3 parts ketchup to every 4 parts mayo.

4. 3 parts honey to 16 parts mayo.

5. 16 parts mayo, 12 parts ketchup, 4 parts mustard, 3 parts honey.

6. 6.

7. 105 ounces.

8. mayo: 2; ketchup: 0; mustard: 0; honey: 1.

THE FISH PEOPLE (PAGE 88)

1. 1.

2. 4.

3. ENOUGH.

4. Mrs. Tuna.

5. 1.

6. WAY TOO MANY. Up to now there are 4 people in the Tunas' boat. TOO MANY, or 6 of the Perches, will not be able to join the Tunas in their boat. NOT MANY, or 1, of the Perches can join the Tuna. This tells you that there are 6 + 1 Perches, to make a total of 7.

   The Perches could also give one person to the Tuna's boat (1), fill another boat (5), and have NOT MANY, or 1 person left over. 1 + 5 + 1 = 7, which verifies that there are 7 Perches.

7. 2 boats, with 2 Fish People left over.

8. WAY, WAY TOO MANY.

LIFESTYLES OF THE RICH AND SUPERSTITIOUS (PAGE 90)

NOTE: Students need to have a basic understanding of positive and negative numbers (integers.)

1. 8th.

2. 7.

3. 37th.

4. 27. The floors that do not exist are:
   7's:
   7, 14, 21, 28, 35, 42, 49, 56, 63, 70, 77, 84, 91, 98.
   13's:
   13, 26, 39, 52, 65, 78, 91.
   Twins:
   11, 22, 33, 44, 52, 55, 66, 77, 88, 99.

5. There aren't 96 floors for Maud to go down.

6. Smaller in absolute value.

7. −69.

8. 72.

PROBLEM-SOLVING BASIC TRUTHS

SOME BASIC TRUTHS ABOUT PROBLEM SOLVING:

1. Problem solving is a skill that can be developed.

2. The way to develop problem-solving skills is to solve lots of problems.

3. The more problems you solve the better you become at problem solving.

4. The better you become at problem solving, the more fun problem solving becomes.

SOME BASIC TRUTHS ABOUT PROBLEM-SOLVING STRATEGIES:

1. There is no single "correct" strategy for solving a problem.

2. Depending on the situation, some strategies work better than others.

3. Almost all problems can be solved using one of the strategies listed in this book.

4. Any strategy that works is a correct strategy.

SOME BASIC TRUTHS ABOUT GOOD PROBLEM SOLVERS:

1. Good problem solvers get good by solving a lot of problems.

2. Good problem solvers learn from answers.

3. Good problem solvers learn from watching other people solve problems.

4. Good problem solvers use whatever strategy works.

5. Good problem solvers seek help when they are stuck.

6. Good problem solvers ask questions.

7. Good problem solvers are not afraid of asking "dumb" questions.

8. Good problem solvers often rework problems, especially those that they fail to solve the first time.

SOME BASIC TRUTHS ABOUT PROBLEM-SOLVING PROBLEMS:

1. Most problems resemble some other problem.

2. Unfamiliar problems always seem more difficult than familiar problems.

3. Familiar problems always seem easier than unfamiliar problems.

4. The more problems you solve, the less likely it is that you will run into problems that are unfamiliar.

5. Some problems have more than one answer, no answer, or require additional information.

TOP 10 WAYS TO GET UNSTUCK:

1. Re-read the problem.

2. Modify your strategy.

3. Change your strategy.

4. Combine your strategy with another strategy.

5. Look at the problem from a new perspective.

6. Look at the answer.

7. Look at other similar problems.

8. Get help.

9. Wait awhile and try again.

10. All of the above.

TOP 10 REASONS FOR GETTING STUCK IN THE FIRST PLACE:

1. You tried to rush through the problem without thinking.

2. You didn't read the problem carefully.

3. You don't know what the problem is asking for.

4. You don't have enough information.

5. You're looking for an answer that the problem isn't asking for.

6. The strategy you're using doesn't work for this particular problem.

7. You aren't applying your strategy correctly.

8. You failed to combine your strategy with another strategy.

9. The problem has more than one answer.

10. The problem can't be solved.

TOP 10 WORST PROBLEM-SOLVING HABITS:

1. Trying to do it all in your head; not writing anything down.

2. Arbitrarily choosing a strategy.

3. Staying with a strategy when it's not working.

4. Giving up on a strategy too early.

5. Getting fixated on a single strategy and trying to use it for everything.

6. Not asking yourself: "Does this make sense?"

7. Being afraid to ask for help.

8. Not checking your answer.

9. Not noticing patterns.

10. Going through the motions instead of thinking.

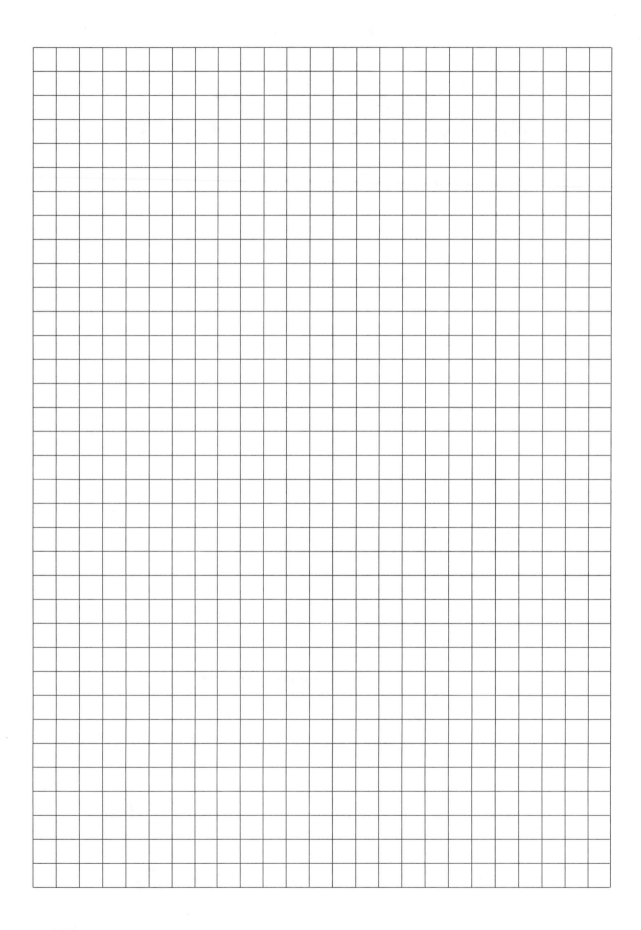